THE PERPETUAL ENDING KRISTIEN DEN HARTOG

KRISTEN DEN HARTOG

THE PERPETUAL ENDING

Alfred A. Knopf Canada

PUBLISHED BY ALFRED A. KNOPF CANADA

Copyright © 2003 Kristen den Hartog
Drawings copyright © 2003 Janet Hardy

An earlier version of chapter seven appeared in the
December 2000 issue of *Blood and Aphorisms*

National Library of Canada Cataloguing in Publication

den Hartog, Kristen
The perpetual ending / Kristen den Hartog.

F
DEN

ISBN 0-676-97457-0

I. Title.

PS8557.E537P47 2003   C813'.6   C2002-903076-5
PR9199.4.D46P47 2003

First Edition

www.randomhouse.ca

Printed and bound in the United States of America

2 4 6 8 9 7 5 3 1

1038 2023

On the day when you were one you became two.
But when you become two, what will you do?

—*The Gospel of Thomas*

PART ONE **EUGENIE**

ONE AND TOTHER

They were twins born seamless, joined up the sides of their bodies. And yet they were very distinctly two. Four arms and four legs, two heads of yellow hair. One loved the water and Tother did not, and that caused the skin between them to stretch and stretch. One always pulling, longing to swim. But Tother was afraid of water. Both its choppy waves and its calmness. Not knowing what lurked beneath.

"Come on!" One whined, because the sun was high and the air was thick with its heat.

But Tother shook her head. She dug her feet into the sand, searching for coolness there. And One kept pulling, walking away. The skin stretched and stretched, strangely painless. Tother put her hand on that bond of flesh. She felt it grow thin, the skin of an onion.

One was at the water now, a toe dipping in. She was looking back and laughing.

"Come on!" she cried again. "It's warm! There are little minnows swimming!"

Tother stepped forward and back, wishing to want but not wanting.

"No," she said. "Come back."

The skin between them turned fine as a web. One had never before stretched so far from Tother. Tother dug her toes more firmly into the sand.

"Come back," she said again.

One, defiant, ran splashing through the water. It stole her legs, her hips, her torso, which once had grown from Tother. She dove and reappeared, laughing still. Wet were her clothes and hair.

"Watch!" yelled One. "Watch how long I can hold my breath!"

And she disappeared into the blue, which was not the see-through blue of sky but the dark and muddy blue of all things lost and searched for.

Tother waited. She watched the vast surface of the water, but One did not appear. Beads of water sparkled on the thinning web just above the place where it disappeared into the river. The bloated sun began its long slow slide. It sat blazing calmly on the water, and then was gone.

Still Tother waited. It might be that One could hold her breath a long, long time. Or that One could breathe in water, like a fish or a mythical mermaid. Tother didn't know. Tother had never been in the water.

She looked and looked for the moon, for the many stars and that brighter one you could wish on. All that came was a dome of black, which meant rain, so she crept beneath the shelter of a tree and listened. Soon the sky was crying on the leaves above her, on the sand, on the water. Adding water to the water One swam in. Tother wrapped the web around her finger, a string to always remind her. She let the blacker dome of sleep engulf her, and though she had never in all of her years slept alone, she slept more deeply than she ever had before.

When she woke it was clear blue morning and the web had become a rainbow that grew from her side in bands of every colour. The bands wrapped around her finger, then reached high into the sky, arching over the water and down again. Tother stood and began to walk in the wet sand that edged the water, winding and winding the rainbow that would lead her to One, though she knew not where.

CHAPTER I SIAM

Look, Eugenie—from here I can see us so clearly that then turns to now. We are eight years old and we are wearing our blue plaid coats with the enormous purple buttons, given to us by our grandparents, who want us always to look identical. For them it is our sameness that makes us special. All they see or understand is that we are a unit: twins. This will never cease to be a novelty— strange, and therefore alluring. Yet for us it is merely ordinary. The strangeness will come later—all too soon—when we two become one, which is me.

But we are not there yet, we are here, and happy, winter-walking with our mother. We look identical, but despite our coats and our grandparents' wish, we are not. Instead we are exact opposites, each the mirror image of the other. One hundred per cent different, and yet you are who I see to a tee in a looking glass. My dull blonde cowlick on the left reflects yours on the right, though today they are covered with hats of blue plaid. The hats and coats cause everyone to stare at us, a double oddity, even more than usual. Strangers gawk at our bizarre inverted sameness, which we do not find bizarre. Our mother would never dream of making us dress this way were it not so brutally winter. Just now there are no other coats that fit us, though she promises soon there will be. Seeing us through my grown-up eyes, I don't mind what we wear, as long as we are warm and safe. From here there is no sign of what will come or even of what has been already. There is only us and her, out walking.

I could get lost in watching us walk in the snow with our mother. We call her by her given name, Lucy, because it is what she prefers, and though we are too young to ponder such a thing, it's true that "Mother" does not encompass all of who she is. Today she is a shining jewel in the snow. We imagine she can be seen from the planes that fly overhead, that a bird could spot her from Timbuktu, with her long orange hair flowing out from her clashing red hat and her coat that is all made from patches. She has her skinny arm outstretched, her pink mitten pointing at a line of white that arcs the sky.

"See those trails? They're like breadcrumbs," she tells us. "So that planes can find their way home again."

We look at Lucy with doubtful faces because it is coming close to the time we cannot believe in stories any longer, especially hers, which are fantastical, over the moon.

"It's true!" she says, laughing. "Look up! That sky is huge, and there aren't any road signs or even any roads."

We look. The bigness of it makes us dizzy. We have never been on a plane, not me or you, not even our mother. What we do not know is that you never will fly anywhere. More than half your life is over, and we have no idea.

"It's really something, don't you think?" Lucy asks us. "How they stay up there, I mean. Ever since Icarus, man has been trying to fly, and all of a sudden it's easy. You can go around the world in a day."

Lucy traces the breadcrumb trail with her finger and tells us that not so long ago, people used boats to get from one continent to the other. It was slow but the only way.

"And most of them didn't go back," she says. "They said goodbye to their families and they crossed the ocean and then they started their lives all over again."

"Like Chang and Eng," you remind her.

"Yes, just like them."

And though she has said a hundred times, you ask her to tell us again why Siamese is the name for them and all the conjoined twins who came after, and she recounts the story of Chang and Eng, fused at the chest, of how they fished the brown rivers of Siam standing up in their boat, leaning this way and that for balance. She tells us Chang's spine grew into a long curve from endlessly holding his arm around his brother's shoulders.

"So they were the first double people?" we ask.

"No," says Lucy. "They were perhaps the most famous, but they were far from the first. Ever since there have been babies, there have been twins like Chang and Eng."

We love these tales, which are happy and sad. Though we are not Siamese twins, we believe the stories say more about us than the blue plaid coats ever can, both despite and because of their inevitably tragic endings.

I look once more at the breadcrumb trail and I think of Chang and Eng, of one hugging the other all the way across the ocean. I am only little in this memory, and I already know I don't ever want to fly. I can see the way the trail gets bigger, and then completely disappears.

You would have loved flying, Eugenie. You liked Ferris wheels and roller coasters and once you swung full circle on a swing set and came out laughing. But I grew up to develop a numb fear of flying, counting the rows between my seat and the emergency exits, so that if we landed and went up in flames, I would not need to see through the smoke and the detritus to find the way out.

As I crossed the sky from Vancouver to Toronto, I counted those rows over and over. I kept my seat belt on the whole time because I knew about crashes, accidental or otherwise. I knew about New York and Peggy's Cove and that Hawaiian disaster, where the fuselage had been torn away in mid-air and anyone not belted in flew out into the sky. Even the flight attendants vanished. Falling through the clouds, which were white air, made from nothing. As the plane began its slow descent into Toronto, I gripped the armrests and thought about the breadcrumb trail that arced through the sky behind me, a tenuous link to Vancouver, which I had tried for so long to call home. Even as I pictured it, that trail was disappearing. Just as you sometimes do when I picture your face, Eugenie, though once it looked like mine in a mirror. I could see my face in the curved window, and beyond it city lights, like stars growing up from the ground. Somewhere in the disarray were patterns: the old and new city halls, the slender neck of the CN Tower, which scraped the sky. I was stargazing from above, in reverse, and for a moment that seemed beautiful, and then not. Though we lived there only briefly, I remembered the Toronto of our childhood, in the 1980s. We lived in Little Italy, you and me and Lucy. Lights in the shape of a boot hung glowing from the lamp posts and swung in the wind. A country within a city within a country. Our miniature home was on Crawford Street, which curved the way European streets do, you couldn't see all the way down it. Everywhere was the smell of smog, of tired buses. That metal smell of streetcar tracks and the sound of wheels screeching over them. We saw vacant faces and garbage no one else seemed to notice. But we had come from such a pristine place—the town of Deep River—that we noticed every messy thing in detail. Toronto was a place where people threw up on the streets, you could sometimes see just what they had eaten, which meant their bodies had rejected that nourishment before it had had any chance to nourish.

I looked away from the window. What I wanted was to stay on the plane and let it take me back to Vancouver, a city that by now had its own problems, although I did not make those same associations when I saw the grey desperate souls who wandered East Hastings Street; it was a city that reminded me of nothing. I wanted to stay on the plane the way you could stay on the subway all the way up to Finch station and then go back the same way. Those faceless trains were amazing. Moving in both directions. Chairlifts do that too.

Remember skiing, Eugenie? We are eight years old and wearing long yellow skis. Our huge stiff boots sparkle silver in the sun. Each of us in mismatched second-hand equipment, our bargain Christmas present. I climb the hill with Dad in a swinging chair with only a bar in front to hold us in place. Because I say nothing, he cannot know how frightened I am. He is not frightened of anything, and I am made from him. I breathe into my scarf, which is hard with frozen snot, and I look down on the shining ice-wrapped branches. The racing-striped toque on my head is too tight, it hurts my ears, itches my forehead. Below is dark and light snow, shadowy moguls, the bright bodies of skiers dipping and swishing between them. I couldn't ever do that. I close my eyes. He is patting my knee now with his gloved hand and in his calm low voice he says, "Press all your weight on your right leg to turn right, your left leg to turn left. It's easy. Snowplow to go slow."

I open my eyes. We're at the top. His hands, which are huge and red, white and blue, are lifting the bar and he is sliding off, placing his skis in the tracks where other skis have been, and I am still on the chair, still sitting, moving forward now, up and away, and as I pass him I catch the look of surprise on his face, his arms held out too late, ski poles dangling from his wrists.

The whole cycle stops for me. You, behind with Lucy, are unafraid and giggling, and that is the only sound other than the faraway swish of skis on hard snow. Your laugh like glass breaking in the cold air, and then silence. I can feel you watching, and all the strangers watching too as I hang ahead of them in the air. My face is chapped. Red from cold, hot from shame. The bar is still lifted, nothing to hold me in place. I close my eyes

against the open space, but the new image that creeps in
is me falling and falling until I land and my skis snap
from my body like bones. The chair jerks and I open my
eyes again. Slowly backwards they move me, everyone
else moving too, even you.

My stomach churned as I recalled gleaming Ontario
winters. How in fall the leaves turned slowly in brilliant
layers and then blew off until hard grey twigs showed
stark against the sky. I remembered that, the turning.
The snow coming to cover the mess of dying. In
Vancouver there was no winter. Fall was rainy but clean,
lasting till spring, which was charming but somehow not
right. With the wind came the damp smell of ocean and
rich wet soil. Pansies bloomed in February. The velvet
petals came in all colours, you could buy them on
Granville Island in black plastic four-packs. Deep purple
or crimson with glowing golden faces.

One year there was a freak snowstorm over Christmas.
So much snow that no one drove anywhere, even city
buses were dormant. No one worked, they walked in
the street, laughing, snow to their knees. They took
umbrellas out with them, thinking snow was like rain,
you might get wet in it. They wore rubber boots or
galoshes, which froze their feet. You would have laughed
to see it, Eugenie. I watched from my window as the
snow fell in enormous flakes, covering the cars. My

neighbour, Mai Ling, had fastened her dustpan to a broom handle in order to shovel her walk. On her head was her Chinese hat worn for gardening. The soft flakes landed and melted on the wide flat brim. I went out in it too, I was elated. So long since I'd seen that blanket. I went with a man I was trying to love—Simon—and we dragged with us a sheet of cardboard, our pretend-toboggan. We slid connected down the long hill of Granville Street in the blue twilight. I remember even the snowflakes being blue, huge and blue and luminous, because Simon had taken a Polaroid of me lying angelic in a snowbank, and the colour had come out wrong. Queer and mysterious, perhaps from the cold, though he had taken the proper precautions and let the image develop in his warm pocket.

Though it made me sad to think of Simon, I tried to stay in that memory until the plane had stopped moving, but the woman beside me was yammering on, speaking to me while the pilot spoke, and the layering of their voices moved like chanting through my ears. Instead of hearing her or the pilot I watched the woman's mouth move, the smudge of lipstick on her teeth. I smiled vaguely and looked away. All sound was suddenly like underwater, muted and distant, as though I was listening in from another time and place.

The plane rumbled along the runway, braking hard and pressing me into my seat. Any time now the pop would come. My ears would clear and the long mumble of voices and noise would cease, and I would be in the world again, this one. I squeezed one hand with the other and swallowed, but there was no change.

Later I was still waiting for it, and waiting for my luggage too.

I stood staring at the long looped belt and watched the belongings of strangers move by. Beside me was that same woman, now sighing in her too-red winter coat. She smelled of musk and wine, the grey beef served for dinner. I could taste that odour. I could smell the conveyor belt too, a rubber-and-motor scent like old cars, and it made me remember another old car, its scabby rust and its muffler, hanging, so I looked again at the woman, whose skin was caked with pinkish make-up, her deep pores and pockmarks accentuated rather than veiled. On her head was brassy dyed hair hard with hairspray. The curls looked shellacked into place. The weave of her bright-red coat stood out like the weave of a Shreddie. She was ready for winter. She had gloves and a scarf in her hands. She was no one I knew, not at all like anyone I had known, and that made it easy, watching her.

The belt went around and around, spilling that odour, and the bulging suitcases were pulled off one by one. Where was mine? I was limp and so tired. I felt as though there were no bones in me, nothing hard to rely on. All I could think was that if I had been able to tell

Simon my story—yours and mine—I could lean against him now. Let his steady heartbeat lull mine as the belt slowly emptied. And then I could lean on him all the way back to my tiny town, the home that came before Vancouver, before Toronto, and it might be easier than going alone.

He would have come with me. For my birthday, he gave me an atlas, huge and too expensive, and under the flap of the cover he wrote, "I want to go everywhere with you." Only that. No *To* or *From*. And yet I hadn't let him come. How could I, when I hadn't ever let him in?

The sighing bright woman reached forward, red lips moving, and she heaved from the belt her huge vinyl bag, the last one. I watched the flat black rubber come to a stop. If my luggage had gone elsewhere, perhaps I should go there too. It seemed like a sign that I should be any-where but here. Maybe I was meant to be in Siam, sucked back into the time of Chang and Eng, those Siamese twins who could never let go of each other. Once they rolled in double cartwheels, but Chang and Eng were long dead by the time we were little girls. And Siam was Thailand now. I swallowed hard to pop my ears but still that plugged feeling, along with a dull ache in each ear. A sign too.

Lucy saw signs, did she still? Omens, she called them, explaining that omens were not always ominous. Dad laughed her off, not believing in good signs or bad. Lucy pointed them out anyway, finding signs in the sky and the water, everywhere she looked. I see us sunning ourselves on the sand at Pine Point Beach. We have been swimming and the hot sun is drying us. We are almost sleeping when Lucy shouts, "Look!" We lift our heads and with our hands we shield our eyes, squint to see what Lucy sees. A frantic something in the water, swimming right towards us, maybe a seal gone wildly astray. Lucy walks to the shore and you and I follow, Dad behind. We are wide awake when we see it is not a seal but a dog with flopping ears, dog-paddling just the way we do when we swim, and he's looking at Lucy. Lucy is wearing her long vermilion sundress, but she wades into the water anyway and scoops him up. All wet, he's wagging his tail.

"Oh my God!" Lucy says.

Now he is licking her face all over. His sloppy pink tongue on her nose and her chin, right on her lips. We don't know where he has come from or where he should go, but Lucy says he belongs with us.

"We'll name him Blue," she says, because he came to us out of the blue, which is true, he did. Blue against her red, red dress is surely grinning, though our father tells us dogs can't smile.

And we have been longing for a dog, that's the one crazy thing. We have asked and even pleaded, but our father has always said no, too much fuss, too much hair, too much smell, too much poo to pick up with a bag.

"We can't keep him," he says now.

"But we have to!" Lucy tells him. "It's an omen!"

Our father groans, and yet he's smiling.

"And who will do all the work, as usual?"

He is trying to be firm, the man of the house, but we can see him soften.

And later it is he who buys the rawhide bones and the basket for sleeping, though the dog never sleeps in there. He curls up on the end of my bed, because my bunk is the lower one. And in the morning he stands right on me, sniffing my face, crushing me. A good way to wake.

Most lovely are Blue's warm, brown, velvet eyes.

Our father always called her omens crazy. Once he called them bullshit, but that was on a bad day so I could not believe he meant it. A potted plant flew from his hand that day, and when the clay broke against the wall the wet soil was like blood dripping. Black blood on a white wall. For me, every outburst was just as shocking as the one that came before. I could only believe that something in him had malfunctioned, that the meanness was not his fault. But you, Eugenie, you never believed that. You were never surprised by his anger, however sudden. Ever since I can remember you held your face in that same non-expression, your little body rigid until his furious tantrum was over.

I saw you in a dream the night Dad called to ask me to come home. Even as I dreamed I felt it must be what Lucy would call an ominous omen, not a good one, because I had not dreamed about you in a very long time.

You were dragging me out of a pool and then you were breathing air into my lungs. I know you know that happened for real, but in the dream it was different because we were as old as I am now. So strange to see you all grown up, not the little-girl you but a mirror image of my adult self. Everything about me showed up in you, except your hair was very long, and also dark from the water. It hung down around my face and grew into my own hair as you breathed. I could not understand what you were doing. I had not been drowning, but with your breath blowing in and out of me I could not make the words to tell you. The ringing phone was a siren. Somewhere I could even see a light flashing, and when I opened my eyes the pink morning sun was shining in. The receiver was in my hand, though I could not recall lifting it. His voice in my ear was a stranger's with the distance of miles and of time, but out loud I said "Daddy?" because he had taken me by surprise. Simon was with me that night, but I did not think of him beside me, of what he might wonder. I listened to Dad tell me all about Lucy. Her dizziness and her mixed-up vision. Whole letters disappeared from the middle of words when she was reading. By the time the tumour was discovered, it was too late. He was calling to tell me. She was lucid now, but she was going. Everything that could be done had been done already, and now there was only the waiting.

"Come home," he said.

When I hung up Simon just lay there looking at the ceiling. He took my hand and let me cry a long while before he asked, despite what he'd heard me say, "Who was that?" His voice was flat, forlorn, as though he already understood I must have been lying to him all along.

I said, "It was my father."

In the airport the attendant sucked a peppermint and seemed not to care when he told me my luggage might be anywhere.

"Might not've even left Vancouver."

His muffled voice and then my own voice, louder, clearer, as though spoken inside my head.

"That would be a definite sign."

I stayed a long while in the airport while they tried to trace my missing bag, but when there was no news, I moved outside and climbed into a taxi. In a way I was relieved, glad to put off the last part of my trip, but my heart was in my throat because all of my stories were in that bag. Not the published copies but the irreplaceable originals, the words written by my own hand, the drawings drawn by Simon's. The first had been *Falling*

Dreams, about a girl named Chloe who was born from the mating of thunder and lightning. She lived alone in the sky and slept on clouds, and every night the clouds vanished beneath her and she dreamed she was falling to earth, where she had never been.

I thought of Simon, all our hard work, our collaborations; of how shocked he must have been when he realized he didn't really know me.

"All this time," he said, "and now you're a stranger again."

He wanted me to talk about my parents, my mother especially. He wanted me to fill in the details of my life, of hers, which was coming to a close, but I couldn't.

"You have to care more than you're letting on," he said, holding my arms and staring into me. "You have to."

Every day he asked more questions, but I remained vague.

"We just never got along," I told him. "I felt like I had no parents, so I thought it would be easier just to say I had none. And then so much time passed. You know, with me and you. It seemed silly to say, 'Oh, by the way. . . .'" I tried to laugh, but I was disgusting myself, and I kept seeing Lucy, who once had been so much more than my mother.

Simon looked stunned. He held my hands and then let go of them. For a long time he looked into my eyes and it made me think of you, Eugenie, and that staring game we'd played, trying to see ourselves in each other's pupils. But Simon remained unaware of your existence, so this was one more thing I couldn't tell him.

He said, "I feel like I don't know you any more."

After that, we never fought. When he looked at me, he rarely smiled, but still he came over every night and helped me pack my things. When he asked why I had to leave altogether, why I couldn't just go and come back, I told him I didn't know how long it took for a person to die. Inside I was crying, but he couldn't know that. He must have thought I was cold, and awful, but he never said it out loud. Once he said, "I should come with you," but I was shaking my head before he had even finished his sentence.

Despite the fact that he was there every night, helping, it felt like he was a million miles away. In silence he labelled all the boxes with thick black letters, *fragile*, *charity*, delicate words. I sat on the floor and watched him pack my mismatched silverware, four egg cups, a battered wok. Other boxes held clothing, a blow dryer, worn towels, the huge papier-mâché doll that had followed me around since I was ten.

He lifted it gently from the box. "Wow," he said. "This is beautiful."

It was the colour of a tea stain and had only one eye. A doll's eye, black pupil rattling in hard round plastic. Once at Hallowe'en that doll had been attached to me.

Conjoined, like Daisy to Violet, those vaudeville twins Lucy told us of.

"Where did it come from?"

It was a perfect moment. He had mellowed and seemed like himself again, the self who loved me. I should have said, "Let me tell you a story," because in my heart and mind I was already tumbling backward. Instead I took the doll from his hands, wrapped it in a towel and laid it in its own box, destined for the Salvation Army. To Simon I said, "It's a long story." Which in fact was not true. In actuality, it was a small, small story.

CHAPTER 2 TWO BY TWO

If I had told Simon the story of the doll, I would have started it here, with Lucy, somehow trying to convey that no mother is more precious than she at Hallowe'en. She invents grand costumes, grander each year, and when we don them we become who we are not. I was a bee the year we were seven, and Lucy fastened gold-dusted baskets to the backs of my knees.

"For holding pollen," she said. "Bees really have those, but they're so small we can't see them."

I was so warm beneath the fuzzy bands of black and yellow, black tights on my legs. You, she made into a butterfly with bright yellow wings, and she gave you a curled drinking straw which you held in your mouth all evening long though it made you mumble.

"That's what butterflies' tongues are like," she said. "Hollow, for sipping nectar." No, she said, they did not always go around with their tongues stuck out, but for some things we would have to compromise.

The year we are nine we are Siamese twins, two sets, which sets us apart.

In the basement of the home we do not know we will soon leave, we watch Lucy bend the chicken wire into the separate shapes of us. She hangs the shapes from the ceiling with fishing line that is nearly invisible, and the bodies look as though they are miraculously suspended in air. Together we dip strips of newspaper into the soupy mixture which is papier mâché and Lucy lays them on with her long thin hands. Her hands are always crumbly with the mixture, as are ours, for we must add many layers so that the flesh looks real.

When the bodies are dry, they are not the right colour and look to have been dipped in tea. Their over-large heads wear yellow hair bought from a store, and in place of eyes they have white circles with rattling black centres that do not always stare in the same direction. Lucy has painted their lips with red nail polish, and now, tonight, we may wear lipstick to match them. The taste of that layer of red on our lips is of wax and perfume, delicious. With string she ties those bodies to our own, and covering each pair of us is one big shirt that smells of our father's skin.

October 31. It is the only one I can remember without going through that rhyme, *Thirty days has September, April, June and November.*

When we are ready she presents us. Down the stairs we come, two by two, each holding another, and he is there with the television on, talking back to the news. What will he say when he sees us? Our four hearts pounding, for there is always the chance for anger, especially now, with our lipstick, which is not the thing to show him. But he is smiling, so nice to see it, and laughing in that way both familiar and strange. There is a light in his eyes that we do not see often. He is taking our picture now, and later, when we see that image of ourselves, each with a twin of our own, we will see him too, in the mirror behind us. One sparkling eye visible, the other hidden behind the camera that captures this moment.

Sideways through the door we go, two at a time. To see you with your twin is hilarious, so big you are now. We walk with them between us, lest we forget they are here. Now they are our centre, and though they divide us, they connect us too. Our steps wearing new paths on the pavement we have so long walked upon. Their paper feet hover just above the ground and their legs do not scissor with ours. They are nothing and everything, light as air. They smell of him and of her crumbly hands, and they may smell of us too, though that is a smell so familiar we cannot detect it at all.

This is the first Hallowe'en we have ever gone out alone. We carry plastic orange pumpkins in which we gather our treats: Smarties, my favourite, the dreadful gummy cheap Kisses and also tiny bags of chips and candied apples. The apples we eat right away. We know he will take them from us if he sees them, that it is for our own good. He fears razor blades buried deep inside the fruit, slicing surprise into our soft mouths. Every year he tells us that story, a true one that came from the TV. If we take the apples home, we will not even be allowed to peel back the sticky Saran, lick and smell the candy coating. It does not matter that the apples are from Mrs. Davies, whom we have known all our lives.

"You're just asking for trouble," he's told us, "if you eat something homemade."

I cannot imagine Mrs. Davies wanting to hurt us, can you? I cannot imagine her playing what he calls nasty jokes or sick tricks. Because he says so, it must be true that some people can be thrilled this way, but Mrs. Davies with a perm in her hair and an old cat named Slim cannot be one of those.

There was that time we were flowers, only six years old, so Lucy came around with us from house to house, remember? I was a dandelion and you were an Indian paintbrush. Our pumpkins were full so quickly we decided to dump them and go back for more. We spilled the treats onto the couch beside him and how giddy we were to see it all there! He was unhappy that night and surely we had not yet seen him that way often. He told us the horrible razor-blade story, and he lifted the wrapped apples by their thin wooden sticks and held them close to our faces. We could smell the sweetness there. They were an uncommon red, deep and shining, picking up light.

The boy in the story had lived in a small town like ours. His tongue and his lips and even the roof of his mouth had split open, spraying blood.

"Never trust anyone but me and your mom—"

"Oh, David," said Lucy, "don't—"

Our father glared at her, and that was all it took to make her stop. He looked back at us and we thought he might resume his story but he didn't.

"Fine," he said. He dropped the apples on the floor in front of us. "Eat whatever you want. See if I care."

We were two drooping flowers. I stood watching him but you turned away. I wish you had seen the electric look in his eyes, which showed not the bored flatness of indifference, but its total opposite.

Now, as Siamese twins, we stand beneath a maple tree, outside of the street lamp's circle of light. All of the dressed-up children float laughing past us in the enchanted twilight. Rebecca is a gypsy laden with jewels. Blue kohl is spread around her eyes in a smoky line and her black hair bounces in ringlets. Evie is a fairy princess in an emerald green gown. Her wand and her tiara, simple aluminum foil, glint as though formed from precious silver. Tonight we can believe in anything. We wish we could stay forever here, leaning two by two against the changing maple and watching this make-believe world.

In the darkness we eat our apples, real-sweet and fake-sweet combined. I have never tasted an apple as magnificent as this one, though the image of the blades that might lurk there is with us always. Will it sneak between our teeth and up into our gums? Will we take a too-big bite and swallow it whole? I wonder will we think of it later, as we fall asleep, not knowing whether it is or is not inside of us?

But it is something else we think of as we lie in our beds that night, you above, me below. All night we hear them fighting, not the words but the thick slur of his voice and then her voice, shrill and nonsensical. Have we started it? Try as I might I cannot remember, did I throw away that sticky wrap? Did you? If we have left those wrappers there in our pumpkins, we have been found out, because he always goes methodically through the foreign things we bring in from outside. And it will be her fault that we have eaten the apples, not ours, though she was not there with us. After all, she was not with us in the spring, when we fell from the tree, and he blamed her.

Truly, though, whose fault was that accident? It was May and we were high up in a willow. Everywhere we stepped we killed a new leaf sprouting. We almost killed ourselves, that was what he said. You broke your arm and I broke nothing. All that showed on me was a small round bruise on my knee, brown, purple, yellow, gone, as though it had never been there at all. Somehow, for our father, that fall was Lucy's fault. She should have had her eye on us at every moment. I brought you home crying, your arm sticking out awkwardly in a wrong direction, the blade of your shoulder a wing. You did not cry but your face was chalk-white and even the blue-green of your eyes seemed paler. Where was he? Working, because someone had to earn a living, and so it was she who took you to the hospital, her hands fluttering around the place that so ached I could feel the ache in my own arm and shoulder and even in my teeth. There was no car. He had it. And no one was home at the next door or the next, I know because I knocked myself, I knocked and pounded. I called Uncle William, and Grandma and Grandpa, but no one was home. And when I asked, "Should I call Dad?" Lucy said no. Her face was white like yours. You were crying so hard that she picked you up and we began walking. All the way she carried you because never had we seen the blur of an ambulance roar through town, and a taxi was something you called for hours in advance. She carried you with your arm sticking out and I walked behind. The sway of her orange hair, unbraided, and your hair too, dull blonde, swaying, thin enough to be see-through. Now you were not beside me. The strangest feeling. With your too-white face you seemed gone forever. On your arm was put a plaster cast, clean and bright white, and my arms remained as they were, just dangling, one at each side. How mad he was to see you broken! Whose fault? Someone to blame. We were to be guarded and she had looked away.

"What is it you do all day?"

Those are the words I remember, the rest the thick slur of his voice. I wanted to stop all his yelling, because I knew whose fault it was. Not Lucy's but mine. I could have said so, but I didn't. I could have told him the truth, which was that I saw you on that branch above me, a stick too slim to hold us both, and I thought, Why should you always be higher? The white of your sneaker was a white I could grasp, and when I put my hand there it wrapped around the branch, and I saw all at once how big my hand was, but still I went on, thinking I could wish myself light and nimble. I saw the rough bark open to the bright wood inside, and when we fell it was you first, then me, my heavy self landing on top of you.

He couldn't know it was my fault. Even Lucy couldn't know. I never told, and neither did you, and so to answer him Lucy said, "They were just playing," because she believed it to be true. "Kids play," she said, pleading for reason. "Kids hurt themselves. Please stop, this is not the end of the world."

And all the while he railed on, just like now. As I lie in my bed remembering the horrible days that match this one, I am learning that every memory has a memory inside it, in the delightful and dismaying way of Russian dolls.

On and on the voices go, the same sounds repeated. *Think of Blue's brown eyes, something nice.* Above I can hear your quiet breathing, not the long relaxed breath of sleeping, but alert breath, tense and aware. Once he was not like this and so there must be the chance that one day he will be that old happy way again, letting us part his hair in the middle and roundly comb the red-brown curls.

I will think of that now, the combing. The smell of his scalp both clean and dirty. There are flakes in his hair that are not in Lucy's, because only men have dandruff. Once, when we combed it that way, he did not recomb it or even muss it up, but left it alone, in the style we had given him, though so ridiculous it looked.

That was the day we rode the winding highway for no other reason than to go somewhere. We half circled Golden Lake, which we could see glinting through the trees, and we sped through Killaloe and then Madawaska, where there was that ski hill now brown and green with its chairs unmoving. It seemed we might go

and keep going and never come back. We did not
know that one day we would go south this way without him, that we might want to leave him behind.

All the way the wind spilled over his hair, pulling
lightly at the tidy shining curls but never quite undoing
the style. Lucy's orange hair was braided and coiled
around itself like a homemade rug. She hummed in her
high off-key voice with the songs on the radio, country
songs that all sounded much like each other but were
beautiful anyway in their magnified melodious way. He
sang too, stretching and twisting the vowel sounds,
making himself American. He could carry a tune. He
could mimic. It was done in fun but joyful to hear, the
mingling of their singing voices knowing each next word.
The volume went up and down, loudened for the songs
they loved, hushed for the ones they did not know. The
music of the cherished songs swelled and filled the car
like something we could feel inside our bodies, dis-
turbing and thrilling, a new pulse, and also something
we could feel in the air around us.

Now through Combermere, with its long and elegant
name that made us think of weddings, suited men, and
across to Maynooth, which conjures mammoth, sabre
tooth. This is less a town than our own town, small
enough to be missed. You could blink your eye, it was
said. North to Whitney meant we were on our way back
in a roundabout way. In his serious voice, un-American,

he said to Lucy, "I wish we could just go and keep going and then come back again."

"*What?*" laughed Lucy. "How romantic is that?"

"To go and keep going?" he asked. He seemed hurt by her reaction, we could see it in his eye, which we watched from the side.

"That part is perfect!" she said. She even reached out and touched his face. "But to just come back again? Where is the romance in that?"

"No!" he told her. "I said, 'I wish we could just go and keep going and *never* come back again.'"

They laughed at that mishearing, but still we headed home. I wondered why it was impossible to never come back, but it remained unexplained except to say that we could not ramble on and on, getting nowhere. Plus the sun was tired now, sinking low, casting a more mellow glow. They could not sing along to the radio forever.

Hallowe'en, and they are not singing now. Their voices this way do not mingle but remain separate, cutting into each other, drowning each other out. Can I drown them both out? There is no place for them in my sleepy mind.

Thirty days has September, April, June and November.
All the rest have thirty-one,
But I don't know how the end is sung.

Here come tears. They spread away from each other on their half-circle paths, moving along the hollow grooves above my cheekbones and under my eyes. I hear them drop into my ears. There is no lump in my throat and so the tears seem just like plain water, without taste or smell or meaning. They come from the ducts in my eyes, two brown spots smaller than freckles, so small they appear drawn on, unlike holes, but that is what they are. Weep holes. Once he had shown us that all the houses on our street had them. "See?" said he. "Every thirty-two inches along the bottom of each house there's a space between the bricks where the mortar hasn't been spread." He went to great lengths explaining, sensing that this was some practical thing he could teach us. "These houses," he said, "they aren't really brick but brick veneer." Under the misleading outer layer they were plain old vulnerable wood. In a howling wet season, the water could seep right through the porous brick and rot the wood inside if not for the weep holes. We looked to where he pointed, and sure enough we saw the precise empty spaces. Since then we have known that even houses could cry.

CHAPTER 3 **WISHBONE**

I took a room in a cheap motel downtown and called the airport so they'd know where to reach me when my luggage arrived. I didn't want to leave Toronto yet anyway. I wasn't ready to see Lucy and Dad. Though I knew that being in Toronto would conjure things that made me feel sick to recall, it was the easy choice compared with going all the way back to Deep River. But already the triggers were coming, and the memories were so vivid that I could feel myself shrinking to child-size, and see you beside me. Even the motel sign, with its burned-out O, sent me flying through time to K-Tel, K-Mart, a plastic world. Those K-Tel records of Lucy's and Dad's, *Sound Explosion, Fantastic*, they held hit songs from the seventies, songs that were long out of fashion by the time we sang them. We didn't know or care. I sang into a huge wooden pepper mill, my microphone. Yours the saltshaker to match. Now they played those same songs on the radio. They were meant to send us back; we were meant to want to go.

The room's walls were fake wood panelling, brown with black grooves and nothing like a real tree. Hung too high was a small painting of a big-eyed girl beneath an umbrella, an over-large robin hovering beside her. Probably there were cockroaches here, the city was full of them. Behind that picture maybe, or lurking in the soap-scummed folds of the shower curtain.

I crept into the bathroom, flipped the light on quickly and waited to see them scurry, but there were none. I shook the shower curtain, checked again for cockroaches and ran a deep hot bath, trying not to think of the other bodies that had washed in this gritty tub which was rough against my skin. Above was a mouldy ceiling. In Vancouver I had a clear shower curtain that quickly clouded with film, but it was only dirt from me, and sometimes Simon. My tub was an old one with feet. It had been my very favourite place to be. Bubbles to my neck, a damp book to read.

The water screamed out of the faucet, and sound-lessly I cried into it. My skin was white and dusty, in places dry to the point of cracking, and it stung as the water rose up around me. I slid down in the tub, plugged my nose, immersed my head. I remembered drowning, and how you saved my life, and then I splashed up, gasping. Out loud I told myself, "It's okay." The thing about memories, though, is that one never knows when they will come, how many or in what order. If only they came bit by bit, in the order we had lived them, life stories would be easier to tell. Easier to bear, too, because we, the tellers, would always be prepared. How is it that a story we already know can so thoroughly surprise us when we recall it by accident? I honestly planned to tell Simon, from the beginning, what had happened to my family, but I could not imagine where the beginning might be, aside from the obvious, the day we were born. True beginnings are more momentous than that. In a way they are a distilled version of the story itself. A parable.

Perhaps here.

My earliest whole memory—one that is not made of fragments impossible to recapture—is of when we are five. It is Christmas and we are standing tiptoe on a stool, helping Lucy stuff the turkey. Here it is, naked, without feathers or a head, but its neck is inside and there are other parts too, mysterious, held in a wet papery bag. Loose flaps of skin cover the holes at each end, and it looks so unlike a real turkey that it is hard to know which end is which. The skin is goose-pimply and in places there are long yellowish hairs. Lucy squeezes with her thumbnails like squeezing a boil, delighting us with disgust. She smears butter on the bird and stuffs it full of cubed stale bread and bits of onion, smelling of sage.

Is it on its back or its stomach? There seems no way to tell. Through the warm window we watch it change colour, its body browning first, then the tops of its foot-less legs, which end roundly in bone. The thin tips of its wings crisp darker than the rest. Nothing takes longer to cook than turkey. All day it fills the house with that smell we can't eat. It is a smell that stays in our clothes and our hair, less pleasant later, but filling us now with hunger.

This turkey was once something living. It had eyes and red feet, wings, though it could not fly. In a book we have, *Farm Animals*, there is a picture of one with feathers, and underneath appears the neatly printed word, *turkey*. I have traced it with my finger and sounded it out for you. Eating a turkey is not at all like eating a cow, called beef once it's slaughtered. Or a pig, called pork. A turkey keeps its name. It is the only being Lucy cooks that stays so close to the way it once was, almost whole. Near the bones are grey veins like our blue ones. Springy and real, where blood once flowed. Still we peel the golden skin. Peel it in long strips and push it hot into our mouths before he comes to carve it.

This is Christmas. Our grandparents, mother and father to our father, come with matching gifts for you and me. It is one of the rare times we see them, though they live just across town. Their uncomfortable presence changes the air in our house, as though strangers have come for dinner. We have to wear shoes. Uncle William is here too, looking silly to us in a shirt and a tie. Already he is an old man, with hair like a cloud that floats out from his head. He is not a real uncle; Lucy says he is more than that, her guardian angel. She came to him as a foster child when she was twelve years old, and later, when we are old enough to contemplate such an idea, it will seem shocking to us that she is not linked to him by blood, by veins. That is how alike they are, right down to their smiling eyes. Of her life before, all she will ever say is "Thank God for William Trillium," which is what she calls him. In this way she is like a character from a fairy tale—Cinderella or Snow White—stemming from nowhere.

Because of company and the season, on the table is spread our poinsettia tablecloth, red and green. A real potted poinsettia sits slightly off-centre to cover a stain we all know is there anyway. It is a stain that has been there for so long we don't think to ask how it came, what made it. This is the day we say grace, which we associate with our grandparents. Now and at Thanksgiving and Easter. Unbearable grace because steam is rising from the cooling food, the dark and white slices of moist and dry meat, the mashed potatoes in which we will form a hollow for gravy.

My father bows his head and closes his eyes, a sign for us to do the same, and before he can speak in those solemn tones, your giggling voice cracks the silence:

Rub-a-dub-dub
Gimme some grub.

"Eugenie!" says Lucy, but she is laughing, she can't not. And if she wasn't laughing out loud, it would show in her eyes, the way it always does. Sparkling blue.

Uncle William grins but our grandmother's mouth is a tight down-turned line.

"This is not the time for goofing around," our father says in his serious voice.

What is this time, so different from the others?

Three ceramic girl angels grace the mantel, each in a pink dress with deep folds as though caught in mid-sway. On their backs are gold wings, so tiny they barely show past their shoulders. Triplet blonde angels with matching faces, though if you look closely, they are different. One with fuller lips. One with bigger eyes. One who seems sad for a reason unknown. Each year these are pulled from a box that says Angels. Unwrapped one by one from the snow of cotton batting.

Christmas, so grace.

Our father glowers slowly at each of us and bows his head again.

God is great and God is good
And we thank him for this food.
By his hands are all things fed
Give us Lord our daily bread.

The food is always less delicious than the yearning. We eat too much, not because it tastes good but because all day we have longed to taste it. Better than the meat is the wishbone, which pulls loose easily if the bird is still warm. It is Uncle William who shows us. Away from Grandma and Grandpa Ingrams and our father, we are in the kitchen helping Lucy clear the mess.

"Look," he says, releasing the delicate bone from the body. It is an intricate *v*, and lovely. "You need to let it dry completely before you pull it apart," he says. "It's important to be patient. Can you wait to do it?"

We nod a promise. We take turns cleaning the meat from it until it is fine grey bone and then we set it on the sill, where the heat from the sun will help it dry more quickly. Every day we touch it. Does it slow the drying, the moisture from our fingers? The dryer the better, the cleaner the break.

And while we wait for the wishbone to dry, the tree dries too. Countless dull-green needles scatter the floor where our presents lay. Those lights—all colours—they are sucking the moisture from this tree we cut ourselves, hewn from the forest outside of town. To find it, we drove in the old rusty car, tires picking up the thick snow and then letting it go again. We drove far down the covered gravel road, as far as we could go, as we will every year, until we came to that fence, and then we parked on the side of the road and stepped out into the bright white day.

On the fence was a sign:

PRIVATE PROPERTY
TRESPASSERS WILL BE PROSECUTED

Long words in big red capital letters. With Lucy's help I could read them, though to you they were non-sense. Our father said in this case it was okay, even good, to break the law, because these trees would soon be cleared to make way for a pipeline.

"All these trees," he said, pointing to a forest that went on forever. "Soon it will be barren land."

I looked at the never-ending forest and wondered which tree we might save. Our father placed the toes of his boots into the metal diamond holes of the fence, and once he was across, Lucy carried us one at a time like baby raccoons to the top, where he received us.

When all four of us were on the other side, we walked and walked. The road seemed the same on this side as it did on the other, but different too, because of that sign and its threatening letters. The saw with its tawny wood handle swung at our father's side.

"That one!" I said, pointing. Snow falling soft on my mitten.

But it was so big he said we would never get it home.

"And even if we did, it wouldn't fit in our house!" said Lucy, laughing, leaning into me.

Again and again I pointed, but I never learned. It was hard to know size in a forest.

"That one!" I said again. "Please, *please*, that one!"

It was a huge white cedar, the healing tree, which I could not have known at the time. What I admired was the flat way it grew its boughs, and the pattern that showed there. Neither needle nor leaf, but a tree of green lace.

"You're crazy," he said. "Whaddya want, to cut a hole in the ceiling?"

Yes, it was what I wanted. If that was what it took, that was what I wanted.

We trudged forward. On our feet were skidoo boots, though we had no skidoo. They were good in the wet and the cold, these boots, because inside were felt booties. But it became so cold that my feet felt bare. The further we went, the further we would have to go back.

You saw it. You went and stood beside it, snow to your knees. It was plain, with short needles. A branch of the ones I had loved.

"This one," you said, touching it. Snow collected on your eyebrows.

It seemed wrong to save such a tiny tree when the big ones were moaning over. He sawed in long movements and soon it came loose, a stick breaking.

It fit in the car between us and the needles scratched against our nylon jackets. Sticky gum oozed from the cut trunk, which was as narrow as an arm, and gave off the fresh, too-strong smell of pine.

Already it is dying, this tree we saved. It will be a whole year before we can save another. On the day it is taken to the curb I am looking into your eye, green and blue, like mine. I can see myself in your eyeball. Separately we wish, holding the slivery bone, which now weighs almost nothing. We cannot say out loud what we wish for because it breaks the spell, to tell, but I wonder, and so do you: Does it break the spell when we cannot help but know? For though we are exact opposites, we have each made the same wish. *Please may we please have a goldfish?* The crazy round-and-round conundrum is thrilling: no matter who wins, surely we can't possibly lose.

I stretched out in a thin towel on the motel bed and looked at a map of Toronto, more complicated than a map of the world. The labyrinthine lines and blotches of colour made me queasy. It shocked me to know that as children we lived among them, if only for a short time. For calmness, I stared at the wide swath of blue along the bottom. Lake Ontario, pathetic ocean.

That spot on the map, it was glowing, drawing my eye upward. It was a line unlike the others, which seemed just like lines, not places. I drew a box around it, Crawford Street, as though it might disappear otherwise. I made myself smile, which had been Lucy's cure for melancholy, and though it was not a real smile, it felt good for a moment. You had a way of grinning. Our small mouths with their thin lips looked just the same when they were closed, but once you were laughing your mouth stretched impossibly wide. Something that stayed hidden in me showed up in your cartoon mouth when you laughed. The giggles rolled out of you, you had a hollow leg where you stored them, that's what Lucy said.

And as I smiled my fake smile, I thought about that, and the bad feeling rose up again, swelling in my stomach. Woven into the pilled pink blanket that had covered so many other foreign bodies was a thick strand of black hair, someone else's. I closed my eyes and pressed a finger against each aching ear. They might pop in my sleep. Hot pain clearing the low mumble, letting sharp sounds in. Maybe my ears would bleed onto the pillow, staining even the feathers inside. That's how they felt, full of blood. I thought of Lucy. Every day her time was running out, and yet the closer I got to Deep River, the less I wanted to go.

I wished Simon was with me so that right then we might make love in a languorous, underwater way. Pale light from the street would shine through the window, turning our bodies phosphorescent. Simon is uncommonly handsome, though his face is round and his hands are too small. It was one of the things I should have told him long ago, but didn't. His imperfections are glorious. The comical swoop of his long broad nose. The space between his front teeth, which showed when he couldn't help laughing at his own bad jokes. That is something, to love even a space.

"This old man, he's been married for years. He and his wife are about to celebrate their sixtieth wedding anniversary, and to make it really special, he wants to take her to the restaurant they went to on their first date, but he is so old and senile he's having troubling recalling the name of the place.

"'Listen,' he says to his wife. 'Whaddya call that flower? Round with lots of petals, prickly stem. Pointy leaves. Very fragrant.'

"'A rose?' says his wife.

"'Yeah, yeah!' says the man. 'Now, Rose—what was the name of that restaurant we went to?'"

Amazing lightness of my arms the day we said goodbye. As he spoke I was aware only of that and of my collarbone, sticking out. I'd become smaller and smaller with each passing day since the news about Lucy. I could circle my hand around my wrist and the thumb and finger overlapped, just like before, when you died. I stopped eating, and it took me years to get my strength back. That bone at my neck a ballerina's.

CHAPTER 4 SEEING DOUBLE

I woke up wondering where I was, who and how old. I lay in the strange narrow bed, not beside Simon, and stared at the stuccoed ceiling. Overnight my ears had cleared like magic. The pain was gone, as was the full feeling of blood collected in there. I could hear the clear sound of my own breathing. The clock ticked loudly, and next door a man sneezed three times. My room had one small window, and the clouds wafting across this morning were cirrocumulus, the happy clouds. They came in rows of small white balls and wisps and rarely made a shadow. Seagulls flew with them, in and out of the frame. Bellies yellow in the rising sun, backs bright white.

I walked to the window and let in the crisp winter breeze, thinking for the first time that the room itself was not so bad. There were no rats or cockroaches after all. Plus this was the top floor, five floors up, so it was relatively quiet and had a view. The window looked south onto the roofs of old buildings and bare trees.

Below I could see Dolores, the motel owner who welcomed me last night as though she'd known I was coming. She called me Jean instead of Jane, and I thought of you, our Gene, our Genie.

Now, in a mauve dressing gown with a parka on top, Dolores shuffled towards the dumpster with a garbage bag in each hand. Her hair hung long and grey, so thin the scalp showed through. She tossed the garbage in the bin, then turned and looked immediately up at me, as though all along she had known I was there. So many eyes hiding in her hair and in her purple clothes. She waved and shouted, "Morning, Jean!" and then she shrugged and held up her hands. "No luggage yet!"

I climbed back into bed and thought about being in bed with Simon, watching him sleep, his mouth hanging open. There is a fine white scar on his chin that shows through brown stubble. He got that falling from the shoulders of a boy named Phil, it has been with him since childhood. I know everything about him. Once while riding his bicycle he swallowed a live bee and said he could hear it buzzing inside him.

I wished to see his eyes flutter open, sleep crusted there.

"Hello," he would say, kissing my forehead. He always said hello when we woke, as though we had been away from each other in the night.

I dozed again, in and out of sleep, and in that drowsiness I recalled that today was Saturday. When we lived here we would have gone to Chinatown to see the strange fruits and vegetables and their Chinese-character labels. I thought about Mai Ling, who had taken my tank full of goldfish when I left Vancouver. Simon simply wouldn't. His absolute refusal had surprised me, but perhaps he had been trying to show his anger about my decision to leave. Fish weren't real pets, he said, you couldn't touch them and get attached. I wanted to tell him how wrong he was, to tell him about our fish, remember? But you were in that story and so I said nothing.

Fish are all we are allowed before Blue. We are seven when Uncle William brings the round glass bowl for our room, so we know it can take a long time for a wishbone wish to come true. Inside swims the fish I call Red Cap, and yours, too, of shimmering gold. You name her Ildikoh, after a pretty girl at school who moved to Renfrew before we could know her. The round bowl is kept on our dresser, Red Cap and Ildikoh floating inside it, nowhere to go but around and around. We want to feed them constantly, and to top up their water, but we have been told already how precarious their existence is. Too much food and they will implode. Too much water will bring them too close to the top of the bowl, and they will jump right out in their quest for a vast ocean. I love Red Cap with his flame of fish hair. He swims to the glass and kisses the image of my finger there, as though there is no barrier between us. I take him out when no one is around, scooping water with him to keep him moist, keep him breathing. Fish breathe in water, people breathe in air. I hold his small cold body soft and hard in my hand. He has no ribs because he has no lungs, but his eyes are like real eyes, he has a mouth and a nose, and all I am doing is looking up close when you catch me. I plop him back in the bowl.

"It was only for a second," I say, twirling my finger in the water.

"Never take a fish out of water," you tell me. They are Uncle William's words. For effect, you add your own theory. "You've probably given him brain damage."

For days I watch for signs of damage, finding none. Red Cap swims and swims, and Ildikoh swims with him, above and below. I sprinkle the food like spices from a tin, not too much, not too little, and I watch the fish rise to the surface, opening and closing their long-O lips to gobble the flakes. But Red Cap in my hand is what I want. I push up my sleeve and plunge my arm in. His vibrant flare of red is almost orange, even out of water. It glows like a halo might, but in daylight too. I lift my hand to my face and smell him. He smells of water, that is all. I put my finger on his lips to make him nibble but he won't.

How long now has he been out? Too long?

I look at Ildikoh, swimming alone. Goldfish are a dime a dozen, that's what Dad says. Red Cap must have cost more but was worth the extra. I touch my lips to him, then slip him back into the bowl.

Is that what kills him, a kiss of death? You find him floating and know it was me.

Chinatown, stinking of a different kind of fish. Layers of them lying grey and bloated on tables in the street. The fruits and vegetables voluptuous, though. Heaps of blushing mangoes. The clean green smell of coriander. A Saturday, Spadina's wide sidewalk swarming with people, the musical Chinese voices loud, then quiet in my ears.

Where is Lucy? We shouldn't be alone here, we aren't old enough. You follow me through the crowd, touching my fingers. I am on constant guard for us, but you, your eyes are roaming, taking in the fruit and the squiggly squid, a pig that has just been hung on a hook in a window. You see a sign that says LIVE CRAB in wobbly magic-marker letters, and there they are, stacked up. Their blue-and-orange bodies are not at all like something living. Still as stones, as shells on the beach. You stop to watch them and I, not knowing, move ahead through the crowd without you. You look up, about to call out to me, and you see how my hand is still stretched out behind me, as though I have not even felt your fingers slip away from my own.

"Janie!" you call, but I move forward.

The throng of people is like water between us, flooding into the space we have created. You know you should swim through them to get to me, but there are the crabs and all the curled-up shrimps beside them. You stand watching for too long, and when you look up again a space opens in the crowd and you see me in the distance, searching for you. Panic, then relief in my eyes when I see you waving. As I make my way towards you, there are people in between us, noticing our sameness. They look from me to you, you to me, as though they are seeing double. This at a time when we could not be more different. Once I am beside you again, irritation prickles off me like static electricity.

"I saw one move his arm," you tell me, pointing to a dying crab. Imitating, moving your arm out slowly from your body, giving me your tortured-crab face.

"They're not arms," I tell you, rolling my eyes.

"*Crab,*" you say and poke me.

The giggles are bubbling up in you. You laugh enough for both of us and I look at you with serious eyes.

"Just stick with me," I tell you, as though I am older. "You know you have a lousy sense of direction."

Now it is you, rolling your eyes.

"We should have a landmark," I say, wrapping my hand around your wrist and steering you down the crowded street, where it is hard to walk two abreast. "Somewhere we can go if we ever get separated."

In the distance is the CN Tower. We can see it from almost anywhere.

"There," you say, pointing. It rises up and up into the sky. "If we ever get separated, that's where we'll go."

CHAPTER 5 FOREVER TOGETHER

"I'm coming," I said into the receiver. "I'm stuck in Toronto. My luggage has been lost."

A pause.

And then my father said, "We're so glad you're coming home. We can't wait to see you."

He was speaking for himself and for Lucy, whom he had loved since he was twelve years old. Remember how he told us? She was spinning in cartwheels across the football field the first time he saw her, a strange, friendless girl, new in town. He said he saw himself in her that day, though we could not imagine how or where, in what part of her electric being he might be found, but perhaps there was something we were missing. Maybe that was all love was—seeing yourself in someone else—

and when love ends, it's only because you fail to see yourself there any more.

That had been the case in the story of Ildikoh, named for a goldfish who was named for a girl. Simon had made the story into such a precious thing. I held the book in my hands when it was finished, astonished by the detail and by the fact that we had made it together. He had given Ildikoh a pop-up unicorn horn and Hal a removable hat. Now I couldn't imagine the stories without his brilliant designs. He may have been the reason the books sold at all, for they had not the appealing black humour of Edward Gorey, nor the romance of Griffin and Sabine. I had written the stories, but Simon had rendered them treasures to touch and hold. For that alone I should have told him where they'd come from. That our father had walked in his sleep, as Hal had. It used to scare me so much to see him in the hall, his big shadow stretched all the way up the wall and across the ceiling. There was a dead look in his eyes. He could look right at us, those times, and not even know we were his, half born from his body.

Ildikoh

This is the story of Ildikoh, who might have been beautiful if not for the many horns that grew from her body. One horn glowed, luminescent and bursting with ESP. It was a gift but not, because with it Ildikoh had the power to know she was unwanted. Oh, she had been painful to bear with all those horns! Nothing but a nuisance to dress and care for. And now, what could she be told or taught that she did not know already? Early on she sliced off that unicorn horn that showed her own past and future so clearly. Smooth pink skin grew over the spot that now held nothing. Pink and then white, shining like a new moon.

Now she was horned, but powerless.

Through literature Ildikoh discovered there were others like herself:

Philadelphia man has nine-inch horn protruding from belly button! Dutch girl has horns for kneecaps! Mind-bogglingly, there's more. . . .

Ildikoh longed to find them. She left the place where she was not wanted and began her search for the place where she would be.

Missing one horn, Ildikoh set out.

What an instant success she was!

What a rising shining star!

Ildikoh made all the papers.

One in a billion! those headlines screamed. *Incredible! Incredible* that she might be something to boast about. *This gutsy gal has horns all over!*

And she made friends, which she had never done before.

And, yes, she fell in love.

Ildikoh had never believed in love before this. She had thought love was a myth. People clung to it the way they clung to God and TV and romance novels because they needed something to believe in.

But here love was. He came in the form of a cowboy, impressively winking with one eye and then the other.

"Hal," he said, putting forth his big hand.

"Hallo," said she awkwardly, wondering at his accent and this strange short form.

The man laughed. "No," he said. "I mean, I'm Hal."

"Oh!" she said. "Hello." She suppressed a giggle. "I'm Ildikoh."

He was huge and splendid, everything a man should be. Like her, he was incredible: one wild ram's horn curled from the top of his head, just a little to the side. He had serious eyes, both blue and green, and he walked in his sleep. Ildikoh walked with him and held his big hand. He lumbered through the streets and once into the ocean and Ildikoh remained a talisman always at his side.

It surprised her to discover that along with love came fear. For the first time since the amputation, she wished for her missing horn. Longing to know about Hal, how happy he would be with her, how long he would stay, if he would be captured by aliens, fall into a manhole or walk away sleeping, never to return. Ildikoh never knowing where he'd gone or why. Would they be forever together? Even without her horn she had a nagging feeling, a sensation that only subsided when Hal woke up.

Awake, when he touched her, he touched all of her horns and his huge hands there sent shivers through her body.

"You have ninety-two horns," he said, after a long silence of touching.

Ildikoh smiled. She fingered the lone horn that grew from Hal's sweet head.

"I used to have ninety-three."

"You do again," he told her, kissing the numb white scar on her forehead and pressing into her.

They were married, Ildikoh in an elegant blue gown and Hal in a huge Stetson that covered his monstrous horn. For this one day, he said, he wanted to be handsome.

Ildikoh was shocked. "But your horn is handsome," she said. She reached under the hat and stroked it. "Why hide it?" she asked.

"I hate it," he said, and the shock of hearing that rendered her unable to respond. The words had tumbled so carelessly from his lips that she looked there, to see if those were the lips she had kissed with her own, if that was Hal's nose above it. When she found his sea eyes she looked into them and was overwhelmed with love and flooding relief. Oh, he had been joking. A joke always showed in the eyes. She did not need her long-gone horn to see into their future. She knew he would always be beside her.

And yet . . . long after the ceremony had ended, Hal's hat remained on his head. He wore it everywhere except to bed. What had changed him, Ildikoh did not know, but she came to love night-time, the only time she saw the real Hal without his hat or his Wranglers or his bollo tie. Even his boxers were gone. She kissed him all over, soaking him up. And when he slept and needed to walk, she walked with him, gently tossing a robe over him for modesty and also dressing herself. If they left the house, he reached for his hat and placed it on his sleeping head before walking outdoors. It crushed her to see that, to know that even in his sleep he was not proud of himself.

Outside, they ambled in silence along Granville Street and down to the man-made island of the same name, where fruit and vegetables were sold in the daytime. It was dark and windy. The smell of aging fruit and of flowers, unseen, was carried by the wind and swirled around them. Halyards clanged against the metal masts of sailboats moored nearby. Ildikoh grew chilled. The wind died and rose again and she felt it touch every part of her face except that one smooth spot, her ESP scar, where now there was no feeling. She heard laughter. A man was approaching with two giggling women, and when they were ten paces away, the man began catcalling.

"Hey, cowboy!" he yelled.

Ildikoh froze. She put her finger to her lips and motioned frantically. "Sssshhhh!" she said, and whispered, "He's sleeping! It's dangerous to wake a sleepwalker, don't you know?"

But perhaps the man was too far away to hear her, since he kept on clowning around. He sang, "Hey there, cowboy, you wranglin' wowboy, you're one tough nowboy, you're cool and how, boy."

It wasn't any jingle Ildikoh knew, but the women joined in and afterwards went limp from laughing.

"Sssshhhh!" Ildikoh repeated. "Please! You mustn't wake him!"

By now the threesome was right in front of Hal, who had stopped walking. Ildikoh looked up at him, at his open sleeping eyes that stared at air. There was a moment of silence as the threesome also took him in. The man waved his hand in front of Hal's blank face.

"Pardner?" he said.

And then the wind came. It blew up a howling gust and knocked the ridiculous hat from Hal's head and was followed by another long silent moment as the strangers stared at his spiralling horn. And then vulgar screeching laughter poured from those three strange mouths. How could he not wake up? Ildikoh thought she saw a flicker in his eye but it was gone as quickly. He began to walk again, tall and proud in his robe, and Ildikoh ran for his hat and then caught up to him and together they strode quietly home.

She lay in bed beside him. She kissed his mouth and tried to let her love flow into him. She was glad he hadn't woken. It could have been traumatic, that's what they always said about waking a sleepwalker. She blinked away the image of that flicker in his eye and went to sleep with her hand on his horn.

In the morning, when she woke, he was awake already, staring at the ceiling.

"Hal-lo!" she said, smiling. Their long-lived private joke.

He turned his head and looked at her. His face was flat and unsmiling and his voice was too.

"Hal is just a nickname, you know. My rugby buddies called me that because they thought they were hallucinating the first time they saw my horn. Hal, get it? Hal-lucinate. My real name is Stephen," he told her. "With a *p-h*."

Ildikoh felt her heart turn over. She tried to say it out loud, *Stephen*, but no sound would come, nor would her lips form the shape of that name. Instead she said, "I never knew you played rugby." Which was sad, but true.

After that, life capsized. Stephen grew despondent, unpleasant. When he walked in his sleep he went fully dressed and kept his hands in the pockets of his trousers, those pockets too small for the horned hands of Ildikoh, and so now she walked beside him, even slightly behind him, for it was hard to keep up with his tall-man stride.

And then there came the day she caught him hatless, staring gloomily into the bathroom mirror.

"What's wrong, sweet man?" It was what she called him because she could not call him Stephen or Hal. The former was a stranger's name and the latter reminded her of the lovely way he used to be—or the way she thought he had been. Either one, too painful.

Now she touched his horn, but he did not respond.

"Yoo-hoo!"

He looked right at her, but was looking right through her.

"I can't read your thoughts," she said.

But she could, this time. Would that she could not.

Oh.

When the doctor removed his horn he was a new man. Rejuvenated, he said, which was not the way Ildikoh saw it. He rubbed Vitamin E cream onto his scar incessantly and went around saying, "Whew, what a load off my mind!"

And he no longer caressed Ildikoh's horns.

"Too bad you've got so many," he said, pointing with distaste. "If you had them removed, you'd be all scar."

All scar, that was how she felt, even though those horns were still on her. Air stung the wounds that love had made, the wounds that myth had made. Oh, how she would miss him.

Not this him, with his creamed head and arrogance, but that him. Her missing horn.

Who would hold his hand when he walked in his sleep? Who would steer him from the ocean?

To herself and to him, she whispered, "Courage, my love," and missing one horn, Ildikoh set out once more.

*

It was strange to think that such a book had made me so close to Simon, and that now we were so far apart. I wrote the whole first draft with one of his good pens. He could tell when I used them, he said I pressed too hard, which was funny, in a way, because remember markers? I always whined to have my own set, complaining that you pressed too hard and spoiled the inky pointed end. You lost the caps too, or chewed them. Left the markers drying on the floor and it was so disappointing to colour with a washed-out red or blue. I should have been able to tell Simon that, to laugh about it with him and let him truly know me. He had asked, "Where do you come up with these names?" and I couldn't even tell him that Ildikoh, the sister of Red Cap, had been my sister's fish. He really should have known that, since the book, in the end, was half his.

I took the King streetcar to nowhere, thinking I needed to be out in the open. But I had forgotten how closed in one could feel in Toronto, even outside, what with all the buildings and the strangers who were everywhere. I stood near the front of the car, hemmed in by the crowd. A fat man pressed into me each time the streetcar stopped. He smelled of pickled onions and his penis was hard. I thought the strangest thing: *Thank God we wear clothes in this society.* As though once I had lived in a place where everyone was naked.

So many high school boys boarded at every stop. They kept cramming on, and each time they fought with the driver about showing their passes.

"Whaddya think you got a pass for?" said the driver. "To fill up your pocket?"

"Hey," said a boy with doggish eyes. "You wanna see the pass, just ask."

"I'm askin'," said the driver.

The boy flipped his pass out of his pocket. "Show some respect," he told the driver.

The driver shrugged. "You got a pass, you show it. Simple."

"Didn't get fucked by his wife last night," said another boy, and the man behind pressed hard against me.

The boys crowded around, more of them at each stop, lipping off. A woman with tight brown curls said, "Watch your language," which made the boys laugh cruelly. One laughed so loud I smelled the gust of his breath when he opened his mouth. He had a thick red scar that ran from ear to ear along his jawline.

"Beg your fucking pardon," he said to the woman.

I wondered if this might become the kind of thing you read about. Things spiralling out of control. Maybe someone would be shot or stabbed. Infected blood spraying onto my skin and hair, so many things to watch out for. I looked at the boy with the scar and wondered what could have happened to him. I thought of the scar on Simon's chin and tried to picture him on that boy Phil's shoulders, laughing before he fell, the look on his face when he knew he would, and I was so caught up in that that it shocked me to realize this boy was leaning towards me, emulating the animated face of a lunatic. I looked away. Shameful to be caught staring. It was one of the first rules Lucy taught us when we came here, *Don't stare.* Always I forgot I was visible, as though cities were like watching TV. And it was easy, now, to forget I could be seen, because you who were with me could not. Together we were visiting the present from another time and place.

Again the streetcar lurched and the man behind pressed into me. He exited when I did, at King and Yonge, and I could hear him behind me, his wheezy breath, his one shoe squeaking. He was following me underground, where first I went with you. I stayed among the throng of boys, who seemed harmless by comparison. Moved swiftly down the steps and onto the train and there he was on the wrong side of the doors, staring at me through the glass.

There was always a creepiness about this city, remember? Even back then, when the city was smaller, to us it was huge, and everyone was someone we did not know, just the opposite of home. I sank into a seat and wished that life had a button for rewinding. If we could find the moment where everything changed, we could go back to it, tape over all that came after.

CHAPTER 6 HALF AS MUCH

You're with me, Eugenie, in our room blue and green like underwater. Smell of sweet lilac drifts in through the screen, so it must be spring. Drooping blooms of frosted purple. Inside, hanging near, is the lamp Lucy made from tissue paper: pasting the tissue paper on, then later popping the balloon. It dangles on a long chain of gold links, and lit it glows blue and green in our blue-and-green room.

We are newly ten in this memory, sitting on my bunk, eavesdropping. Each with a glass pressed to the wall and one ear, turning the glass both ways though one way does not seem better than the other. A last drop of juice drips into my ear.

"No one else will ever love you like I do," he says. It is meant to sound kind, it must be, but she does not respond. It's here that his tone changes. "No one will, you know. Do you know that? Maybe they'll try, but probably they won't even do that."

His slurry voice comes through each glass and into our ears, so clear I can feel his breath there, can you?

Lucy cries. For a long while no one says anything. I look at the blue wall of our room, at a paintbrush hair painted over. I turn my glass.

"I'm not leaving because I want someone else to love me."

"Good," he tells her, making an empty laugh. Now he speaks in his low mean voice, hard to hear though he lets each word out slowly. He says her arms are too long and she's skinny and weird and has stringy hair.

"You'll fit in in Toronto," he says flatly. "Everyone there is strange."

Through the glass I hear nothing and then a sound like crying. It's him. He doesn't know how.

Later Lucy tells us the one thing she wants us to know about love: the very basic rule is that what you adore about someone will one day be the thing you try to change. She uses her serious face and her luminous eyes look at me, then at you.

After a long pause, she shrugs, and says, "Twice as much, half as much." This is splitting up. It doesn't mean the love is halved, in fact it might be doubled, because love for a child—for two children—is a whole different love story. We will live in two homes, she tells us, this town and the city. In a way, we'll be lucky.

She goes ahead on the bus without us. She'll find us a nice place to live, she says, and our father will take us there when it's ready. At the bus station she kisses the tops of our heads, hard. We touch her bright hair, braided in two long ropes, and breathe in her sweet apple smell, and when we look up to say goodbye, she is watching our father, but he sits in the car with Blue, looking elsewhere. Uncle William is here too, he's the only one crying. He holds Lucy in his old fat arms for so long that we wonder if he might never let go. Lucy over his shoulder winks at us, just waiting, and surely loving the pillowy feel and the shaving-lotion smell of Uncle William, as we do. He lets go and kisses both her cheeks with exuberance, and all together we watch the driver smile at Lucy as she climbs on. She waves through the dark window.

Without her we eat canned stew with chunks of bread in it. Another night mushy noodles, also from a can. The house stays dark and quiet, not even the radio on. No longer does our father play the wistful country songs about doomed love, lopsided love. Love is light and heavy, we know that by now. Not an easy thing to carry. He does not even try to carry himself. Can't hold himself up, remember? Drinks from his gleaming flask and sits slumped in his old brown chair, which is frayed at the arms. Barely speaks, barely looks at us, and when he does his eyes waver and move away, as though it hurts to see us, small versions of her, of each other, and the reflection of himself there too.

In the night a sound too loud and long to be crickets disturbs the silence. I wake and tune it in. Lie staring at the ceiling, listening, trying to place the sound, and then I creep out of bed, following it, and Blue follows me. It's him again, crying strangely, doing it wrong. The sound is him ripping the clothes she left behind, things she hadn't wanted anyway. Her purple dress, which came to the ankles, your favourite. I never told you. I knew you could not forgive easily. He starts at the hem and rips it all the way up one side, the seam popping open. It doesn't make him feel better, I can see that. I watch from the hallway, unnoticed. I can smell him from here. There is a vein standing out queerly on his forehead. I cannot recall ever having seen it there before.

This day he takes us to school, but in his wallet there is no money for hot-dog day. Not even enough for one hot dog between us, and today is Tuesday, everyone will be eating them.

We stand and look at him as he digs into his pockets, pulling out lint and the wrapper from a chocolate bar.

"Sorry," he says. "I forgot." His eyes are watery, blue and green like ours.

And then at noon we are in the cafeteria, hot-dogless, and in he comes, so big among the children, shouting, "Hey-hey!" too loudly. "Looky here!" In each broad hand is a hot dog wrapped in silver paper, and as he bends to give them to us, I see that flask in his pocket with the pens, a red and a blue.

How proud he looks, wide smile showing teeth too yellow. *Go away,* we want to say, *you don't belong here, everyone is staring.* These hot dogs are too big, unlike the others, so big they are practically sausages, compensation. And he has loaded them up with onions and pickles and too much mustard, not the way we like, breaking our hearts. Breaking his heart too, I can see it in his face. Can you?

We spend the long hot summer without her.

We have to go next door to Miss Reese's on weekdays while he works, and though Miss Reese is old and has no TV, she has a pool and also a trunk full of dress-up clothes from all the places she has been. There is a snow dome you love, and you shake it while she tells her stories. She says she was a looker in her day, that's the way she speaks. It's hard to see now though. She has a sagging, powdered face and around her mouth there are many lines from smoking. The big ashtray on a stand is always full of crushed cigarettes with their red-lipsticked ends.

In the trunk there are many fancy dresses, of velvet and of satin. Even inside out they are splendid. Not only does she help us try them on, she dresses herself in them too. She is rake-thin, but tells us that once she filled them out nicely.

"When you were Italian?" we ask.

Miss Reese laughs. *"Si,"* she says.

We never would have guessed that once she was Italian. No trace of an accent is left in her voice, which is gravelly from smoking, yet when she tells us what her name was—"Maria Rosa Carmelita Ricci"—and where she grew up—"Roma"—the springing, rolling sounds are like another language.

"Ah, Italia," she says. She leans back in the chair in her too-big red dress and lights a cigarette. *"Bella, bella."* She smokes for a while and looks at the ceiling, and then in her regular voice she tells us, "Pretty, pretty, that's what that means."

"Italy was pretty?" we ask. "Or you were?"

"Both!" she says with her raspy laugh. And then: "I was a goddamned looker."

I am looking at her now. Her eyebrows are lines made with pencil and there is a smear of steel-blue on each eyelid. I can see her bra strap, dingy and grey, sticking out from her dress. I cannot imagine that once she was young. As young as we are, and younger.

She gets out a map and shows us that Italy is a boot with a heel. Across from it is Spain, where she went with a rose in her teeth.

"In your *teeth?*"

"Well, not really," she says, and the laugh that escapes turns to a cough. "But so to speak."

Every night he shows up at five to five and takes us back home again. Just across the lawn, a whole different world.

He makes us take off all of our things and throws them straight into the washing machine because he cannot stand the smell of us.

"You stink of cigarettes," he says. Meanly, as though it is we who have been smoking.

But there is guilt in me. I have come to like the smell. It lingers on my skin and in my hair, which I press to my nostrils and breathe in. Fragrance of Italy, of Spain and red roses.

"Bene," you say, eating Alphaghetti.

We laugh and he looks at us, an eyebrow raised.

"It means 'good' in Italian," I tell him. "Miss Reese taught us."

And now we talk over each other, spilling out all of her stories. The man she loved, the one she followed to Spain. Olives on trees and the sweet fragrance of mimosa, which she even now misses.

He sits and he listens.

All he says is that Miss Reese is full of shit.

I look at the orange noodles in my bowl. The letters there spell stories.

"Come off it, she's not from anywhere but here," he says. "Do you think *Reese* is an Italian name?" He is laughing, but there is no smile in his eye. "How gullible are you? Just ask her how she ended up in the Ottawa Valley."

She has told us already but we simply don't say. It is the best part of the story.

To tell him would spoil the ending.

All that night he is awful. There can be no TV because he has what he calls a splitting headache. It must be the pain that splits him in two, because he is both our father and the meanest man we know. He says even hearing us talk makes his headache worse, that that is all we do, yammer, yammer, yammer, don't we ever shut up. Quiet as mice, that is what we will be. You will lie on the rug with Blue and your comics. I will go in my mind from Italia to Espagna with bangles on my arms.

There is a man I love there, his name is Pablo and he fights with bulls. All he has with him is a sword and a flimsy scrap of crimson silk. It means he is courageous, but I can never understand that, the fighting. How can he be so kind and then kill? I feel sorry for the bull and for the blindfolded horses. I cannot watch his moment of triumph, his pirouette and the plunging of the sword.

And yet he teaches me the flamenco. In his too-small jewelled jacket and boots with heels he dances stomping around me, clapping his hands. I spin. I clack my black castanets. I wish we could forget about those bulls. I wish we could dance the flamenco forever, and I tell him so.

"*Ti amo,*" he whispers.

It doesn't mean "me too" but "I love you," which is not the same thing, and so he returns to the ring and the bull and I am in the stands not shouting "Bravo," because how can I, knowing the perpetual ending?

But I do not know everything.

There is the wave of the silk and the roar of the crowd and I lower my eyes with their long black lashes. My castanets are in my lap, a picture of a man and a woman on each. I am watching them when the roar becomes a gasp and then silence. Crimson flows from him, my dancer.

"After that I just wanted to get away," said Miss Reese, shrugging. She lit another cigarette. Smoke came out with the words she was speaking. "I closed my eyes and put my finger on a map of the world, and there it was, Deep River."

I wish he could have waited for that part. It's because he is downhearted that he didn't. I know it. I hear the muffled sound of his crying after he puts us to bed.

Nights, we miss our mother.

Instead of Pine Point, on weekdays we swim in Miss Reese's pool, which is almost better. Blue is not allowed in, he has to stay tied to a tree. Miss Reese says his fleas will spill into the water, that she doesn't want to get bites. She doesn't swim though. She lies on a lawn chair in her bathing suit and oils her drooping skin. I wonder how it can happen, that your skin gets too big.

There is a smell to chlorine. The pool turns our hair to yellow straw and whitens the whites of our nails. Miss Reese says this see-through turquoise water is better for us than the dirty old Ottawa River, where you can't see what's floating in it or lying on the bottom.

"People pee in the river," she tells us.

That we know, we have done so ourselves. You can't pee in a pool, though, it makes a stream of yellow in the water and everyone can tell it was you. This might be a rumour but we don't take the chance. We simply swim and jump from the diving board, and then we lie on the hot white pavement and then we swim again.

Miss Reese calls it hotter than Hades this summer. She says it was hot in Italy, in Spain too, much hotter than here. But she's what she calls an old gal now, and she can't take the sun the way she once could.

"You should've seen my tan in my Mediterranean days," she says, running her hands over her legs. "I had an olive complexion. Now look."

The skin is white and blue, but it is better than green, is it not?

She sighs and fans the air with her hand. "Ready to go inside?"

But we have only spent moments, it seems, and so we beg to stay longer.

"Listen," she says. "I'm so hot I'm dizzy. I've got spots in front of my eyes. You little mermaids swim on, but I'm going in."

She says that she'll watch from the window, and she does, sitting in the big red chair with the fan blowing on her. But soon she is sound asleep, her mouth open and her head lolling back, and that's when you point to her cigarettes.

"Let's," you whisper.

Dripping wet, we light them, many strikes to get the flame. The smoke is like a blade inside, and the taste is the smell of Miss Reese. I feel as though my head has been lifted from my body. I am heavy and light and laughing. I am watching the blue smoke billow from your mouth and thinking I'd like to dive and not jump from that board in spinning somersaults, and that is where I am next, on the board, in the air, in the bleaching water. I hear my head hit the aqua-blue bottom and feel a flap of skin tear away. Redness swims by me in a cloud and the ripped place stings like something burning. I see my seaweed hair floating out from me and then I see nothing. And when I wake I wake to your hot breath, smelling of stolen cigarettes and warm lemonade.

Everything and nothing has changed.

This cut, it's not deep enough for stitches.

"It isn't really even a cut," you say, inspecting. "Only a scrape."

There is no sign of blood in the water. Miss Reese in her chair is still napping.

"If she notices the scrape, we'll just say you tried a dive and hurt your head," you tell me. "Not the CPR part."

CPR. It means cardiopulmonary resuscitation, a thing you cannot hope to spell, but you know how to do it, the opposite of me.

"Okay?" you ask.

You've got me by the arms and I'm nodding.

"Okay," I say.

We won't tell anyone you saved my life.

Summer stretches on without Lucy, but there are delicious moments, made vibrant by the knowledge of my death and resurrection.

Saturdays, Uncle William collects us and brings us to his ramshackle house by the river, just at the edge of Pine Point Beach. There is a huge rhubarb patch here, in his backyard, and we may eat as much of the sour treat as we wish, dipping the long red stalks in sugar. Like celery, the rhubarb peels off of itself in curly strings.

Though we love Miss Reese and, of course, our father, we wish we could live out this summer at Uncle William's. Day and night the windows are open and the back door is kept ajar with an old shoe. Wind moves through the room in a summer-breeze circle. Only when it is raining are the windows pulled almost-closed, and then we are three caterpillars in a William-Trillium cocoon, hearing the rain on the red metal roof, and seeing it teem into the river.

These indoor days we spend in a kind of aviary grave-yard, for Uncle William has a room full of birds that lie as though sleeping in a cabinet of wooden drawers. This is a collection he began as a much younger man, when he first arrived in the Ottawa Valley.

"But why?" we ask. "Why would you?"

All he tells us is that birds, living or dead, intrigue him. He says the way their legs bend, the way they are covered in feathers, make them seem as though they are relics from a different world and time. We look and look but cannot see that. They are birds, after all. Ordinary robins and grosbeaks. For me, what is intriguing is the cabinet as a whole, the way every drawer holds a perfect sleeping body, the way we are permitted to peek in on that sleep.

On the stick leg of each bird is a paper anklet telling not only the name of that bird, both Latin and common, but also where it was found and when. Some of the birds arrived long before Lucy did, such as his first, a treasured blue jay from 1953. Uncle William's love for all living things is so enormous that it extends on into death, or the afterlife. In order to keep these birds in their serene state of sleeping, Uncle William has carefully prepared the skin and the bones. It is hard to believe, looking at them, that their flesh-and-feather suit has been entirely removed and placed back on them again.

To us, they are feather dolls. We pull the drawers open in silent awe and regard the little bodies. There is a feeling that rises up from the birds and down into me, of calm and of rightness. The ones who are made of the most muted colours—grey and sand and fine powder blue—fill me with this tranquillity. And though I cannot yet articulate such a sentiment, I am learning there is grace and dignity in the way something is cared for, admired, even after it dies. The paper anklets are tombstones, in loving memory.

I am aching to bring someone here, to let an outsider into this special bird world, and I choose Rebecca, one of the few girls from school who likes me better than you. Before she comes, I imagine her seeing and loving the birds, even stroking them with her finger, and then reading with me on the beach, not in the hot blare of the sun but in the rustling green shade of a maple tree. From time to time I will read my favourite parts aloud, and then Rebecca will, and the rest will be merely the sound of the waves and the leaves.

So rarely do things unfold in the perfect way of dreams. Rebecca screams when she sees the birds. No matter which drawers we pull open, Rebecca squeals and laughs in revulsion. I am so dismayed I stop showing her anything at all, but you, Eugenie, are delighted. You open and close the drawers so rapidly that the birds rock in their eternal homes and the whole cabinet is jiggling.

Uncle William comes and all he says is, "It's such a nice day, why don't you play outside?" though surely he is disappointed that his birds have been so uselessly ridiculed.

Outside it is me lying alone reading *Anne of Avonlea,* while you and Rebecca paddle Uncle William's canoe in a back-and-forth zigzag from the shore to the raft. I watch you in the sunshine and I wonder, Would it have been different if today it had rained? Could the sound of the drops on the roof have the made the birds more touching?

What is so surprising is the certainty with which I believed Rebecca was more my friend than yours. The only one other than me left standing in the spelling bees at school. Your laughter lifts off the water and mingles with hers, making a song only half-familiar, thus strange, and I recall with hot humiliation that once a girl at school revealed a trick to tell us apart. "The one laughing will almost always be Eugenie."

CHAPTER 7 **FROM ME TO YOU**

August, the twentieth day, when finally we leave for Toronto.

Uncle William once more cries freely, and Miss Reese tells us she believes we are going on a great adventure.

"There's nothing like seeing the world," she says.

She leaves lipstick traces when she tells us goodbye. There is one on your cheek and there is one on mine too, I can feel it. For going away, she gives me her castanets, and I hold them one in each palm, rubbing the smooth curved shells. To you she gives that snow dome you were always shaking. A little person inside in a coat and a hat, so strange to see in this heat.

It hurts to say so long to her, to Uncle William and Blue. They stand in our driveway, seeing us off. We ask as a last wish that Blue might come with us in the car but our father says no and gives no reason. I hold Blue's paw in my hand and touch the chapped pads and you kiss him right on his dog-lips when our father isn't looking.

And so we go to Pembroke, me in Lucy's seat. He can't drive us all the way, he has a job, you know, he can't just take off whenever he wants. What we can't believe is that he is letting us go alone. Right until the day we leave we are sure he will change his mind. We drive without the radio on, and never have we gone anywhere in silence before. I wait for him to turn the car around and take us back home, but he doesn't. In my head I sing radio songs, all the words memorized, a way to learn sorrow. The trees blur by as though they are moving, we are standing still. Once a leaf blows in with the fresh hot air and you catch it in your hand, so surprised you let go too quickly and the wind blows it out again.

And in Pembroke he stands and waits for the bus with us, keeps the car running. He pushes a crisp new map into my hands and you lean over my shoulder, looking on.

"Find your street," he says, eyeing the highway. "You gotta know your way around a place like Toronto, it's not like home."

I unfold it, that maze, all scribbles, nonsensical. More complicated than a map of the world. I stare at the wide blue bottom to calm myself. Lake Ontario. Maybe we can go there. I fold and refold the map, trying to get it right, until finally he grabs it, exasperated, and makes it small again.

Oh, he is hurting, do we even know?

We board the bus and I can see him talking to the driver in that way he has, with his face too close and his voice all pushy. He is making sure we will be cared for, that's all, but I am hot and embarrassed, I don't want to see. When the bus pulls out, we don't wave goodbye, I because I can't look, you because you're looking forward. Our father in the fading periphery.

We are small-town twins from a town with no mall, no traffic lights even. Our bulging suitcases ride beneath us, rubbing against the belongings of strangers. Eight-hour milk run, the air thickening with the stench of breath and toilet, bags of Cheesies. In the next town we have to show our tickets again, and you've wrapped a huge wad of pink gum in yours, stuffed it down the crack of the window where stale air blows. You pull it out and present it, giggling, and despite his serious uniform, the driver cannot resist smiling at you.

We drive through towns like and unlike ours, heavy with pine trees, then brightened by the too-thin trunks of birch trees flashing white. Plaster casts of the forest. More people climb on and now we laugh at them, because with him gone, with us gone from him, it's easy to laugh. Those people, they're hicks. Tiny minds from tiny places. We can tell they're stupid by their outfits, and if they say "Gidday" to the driver, we laugh out loud. We're reforming ourselves, shedding a skin. Good riddance, Deep River, we were drowning in you! Good riddance, Pembroke, which calls itself a city, and Bancroft, and even Wilno, where once the Pope visited.

"Only Polish people live here," you say as we ride through.

Once we visited here with our parents, a family excursion, though we were not Polish or even Catholic. That was a paradise day. The summer wind blew us down the winding highway and the radio was singing. At Wilno we stood at the lookout and looked out on the many descending layers of hill and trees. The famous church was behind us, high above us, drinking in the same view. It was easy to see why a Pope might come to such a place.

"Boring," you say of this ride, and out loud I am quick to agree, it's nothing new. Nothing but gas stations and doughnut shops, men with John Deere caps perched too high on their greasy heads.

Close to the city the air changes, a new smell in it not from nature, we detect it even inside this bus. The highway widens and that seems strange, to travel with cars beside us going all in the same direction. To the left and to the right, buildings of gleaming blue glass grow from the ground. In the sky hangs a humid layer of yellow.

When we arrive at the station she is there, looking like she belongs. A new outfit, cityish, but old too. Someone else's.

"I got it at a second-hand shop," she says, twirling, showing a red skirt with a pink skirt beneath. "It looks a bit Spanish, don't you think?"

It does, we know it. We tell her about Miss Reese and the tragic matador.

"When I was a girl she was half-Japanese," Lucy tells us.

We had forgotten that we know this story, of Miss Reese and of origami, of how, if not for Miss Reese, Lucy may never have longed to make things with her hands. But art is more than origami, it's why we're here. Lucy works at a drugstore now, she tells us, but it's only to pay the rent, to pay for the courses she'll take at night, not just in painting but in sculpture too. Perhaps even in the grand-sounding history of art, of which admittedly she knows little. But she will know plenty, some day.

"Here you can take a course in anything," she says.

Art makes us uncomfortable, though for her beloved sake we do not say. We think of the long-buried pig's head, which might somehow turn up again now that we are away from home and from him, free to do as we please. We were seven years old in her bone phase, which began when she found a mysterious white bone on the beach. She stroked and stroked it, admiring the yellowish white and the weightlessness. She kept it on the sill in the kitchen and soon her collection grew to include a chicken's wishbone, smaller than the turkey's we had wished apart, and also other bones not meant for saving, both the leg and the wing. He said it was starting to look gross, like a witch's kitchen, but she laughed him off and left them up. She said with a serious face that the curve of bone was pleasing. She even tried to show him but he would not be shown. Still, he might not have minded had she left it at that, a collection that fit on the window sill, but we can remember the pig roast next door, and the pig going round and round. We watched the creature darken and crackle through the slats of our fence. People ate from his body, even though the remaining whole was right there in front of them. Parts of him were carved off and served up and the rest of him stayed, turning slowly. A long metal pole ran through him. Lucy watched too, she came to pull us away, but when she saw the pig and the people, she was transfixed. Her mouth fell open and hung there.

Our father was appalled too, because we were staring.

"Goddamn it, mind your own business!" he hissed.

He pulled us away from the fence and shooed us into the house.

That night, in our room, she said she thought it was wrong. She said she wasn't yet sure why, what the difference was between cooking up pork chops and roasting a whole pig, but she was sure there was a difference and she wanted us to know. She said she was going to get the head and make something out of its bones, that it would be part of her collection.

"What can you make out of a pig's head?" we asked.

"I don't know," she said. "I only know it makes me feel like making something."

"But what can you make out of bones?" we asked.

"Art," she said. "I hope."

How she got the head we do not know. What she wanted for her art was the bone, not the burnt florid face or the pointing-up ears. Not the thick eyelids, singed where the long blond lashes had been, but the base itself, stripped naked. She said she had put it somewhere safe to let the flesh fall away, to let the maggots eat it clean, that she was only telling us so we would not be alarmed if we came across it. We were sick with worry. Every day we waited for that grisly discovery—not by us but by him. Somehow we knew it would be him.

It was night when he found it. We had been sleeping soundly and his yelling woke us up. He bellowed, "What's the matter with you?" but it was not in any way a question. We listened to her crying, to her feeble explanation, which even to us had been bewildering, and we waited for it all to be over.

In the morning every bone had been cleared from the sill. The wood had been wiped free of flies and of dust and the glass behind had been cleaned with Windex. Lucy made us eggs on toast, our favourite. Her face wore the tender smile that came when she was hurting.

The bus station is palatial, two levels, filled with travelling people, and over the P.A. a man calls out the names of places we have heard of but never seen. Niagara Falls and London. Windsor. From here you could go anywhere, Miss Reese was right. At home the bus station is in a gas station, you wait on the highway's shoulder if it's closed.

For a treat, Lucy buys us French fries with gravy and we sit in the bus terminal, watching. As we eat I hook my leg over my suitcase because our father told us to watch out, thieves are everywhere here. I have to keep my eye on your things too, her purse, which you both let loll beside you as though they are unnecessary. But the French fries in their yellow paper dishes are delicious.

On the streetcar we stand with our flowered suitcases between our legs. All the seats are taken, there is no room for us. The city was full before we got here. It is rush hour, Lucy says, and everyone is rushing home. This is our home too, Toronto. Everywhere I turn there is something I have never seen before, and thus holds no meaning for me.

One thing that will never change, no matter where we go, are the ever-staring eyes of strangers. They look from me to you and back again. They nudge their friends beside them. We are so accustomed to this that we barely notice at all. Only later, in the infinite absence of you, will I recall the bold stares, and then because they stare no longer.

Our home, when we arrive, is crooked. It has a square brown lawn where even dandelions don't grow. Our place is the basement only. Never have we lived in part of a house before. Lucy calls it a flat because she likes the word, it's English. *Flat* sounds flat to me. Flat voice. Flat pop. Flat broke. Flat chest. You, whispering, call it a hole in the ground.

"Like ants," you tell me. "That's how we'll live."

There are only two rooms plus the bathroom, as small as a closet and with a green tub. Lucy's is the little room beside that, and for us she has set up beds in the living room.

"Just you wait—we're going to make pulleys for them, the way Emily Carr did with her chairs, so we can raise or lower them as needed." She claps her hands and grins at us. "For now, it's like a motel—think of it that way," she says. "Something different—a real adventure."

We don't respond. We look all around, up at the ceiling, where the mysterious pulleys will be, and then back at the beds, which are not even bunk. It is different, all right. I wonder what he would say if he knew we were to sleep in the living room. I assume you are with me in my loathing of this place, but I look and see you smile.

"We wouldn't ever have to make our beds—we could just stuff all our junk on top and pull them up!"

"Sure," says Lucy. "Why not?"

I can think of a million reasons—the absolute wrongness of mess, also the weight and the danger of the suspended beds falling—but when I list them, Lucy shrugs them off.

"The man upstairs is so fat," she says, "that if the ceiling was ever going to cave in, it would have done so by now."

On this, the first night, I lie looking at the window. It is closer to the size of a dollhouse window than to the size of our windows at home, which push out into the sky when opened. You, too, might be looking at the window, but the room is too dark for me to know. All I know is that you aren't sleeping, I can tell by your shallow breaths. The man upstairs is walking back and forth, back and forth, and I wonder if, he never stops, will he wear out the floor and fall through to us?

Your voice comes through the darkness in a sleepy nonchalant whisper.

"I think there's a ghost in here."

"It's him," I say. "Upstairs."

"No, not that. This is something else."

I feel a chill spill through me. I try and try to feel the ghost, but nothing is there.

"What do you mean?" I whisper.

You sigh a sleepy sigh. "Somebody's here with us."

And then, as though you don't even mind, you are snoozing. I hear your breath deepen and sense you leaving, and I remain wide awake, wondering where a ghost comes from, and why. What it might do. I think of Ouija, and how we sat with the board between us, asking when will we die or be kissed. You said a ghost moved our hands across the board, and it seemed both true and untrue at the same time. Like a ghost we could manipulate, a spirit who lived in the vibration of our fingers. Such a ghost disappeared when the lights came on, when the lid of the box closed over the board. But what of this ghost, whose presence is a mystery to me?

In the days ensuing, I discover that the man upstairs is fat, but he is not fat enough to fall through the floor. We often see him in his worn undershirt, taking garbage to the curb. Our ceiling, his floor, creaks where he walks, so we know where he goes at all times. We can hear his toilet flush and the voices from his TV, his voice too, talking back, the way our father sometimes does. Lucy says the cockroaches come because the man doesn't keep his place clean enough. They don't know the difference between our place and his, only that if there's something to eat up there, there must be something to eat down here too. "Roaches," she calls them, a familiar short form.

The two windows, one in the door and one high on the opposite wall, bring less light than a fingernail moon, but at the right time of day the room glows golden. Lucy has painted all the walls and even the ceiling a colour called clementine. She says we'll need that, the brightness, and then she croons that song we have always known, dreadful sorry Clementine. All the oh-my-darlings sound wrong without our father's trilling voice mingled with hers, because his is the beautiful one, she is out of key without him. She is using her jokey voice, which she always uses for songs like this, but it is not until "lost and gone forever" that I realize for the first time what a crying lament this is, about a miner forty-niner and his daughter Clementine.

Ruby lips above the water
Blowing bubbles soft and fine
But alas I was no swimmer
And I lost my Clementine.

As yet, there is only one picture on the wall, and it is not made by Lucy. Lucy says it is not merely a picture, but a picture of a sculpture, something more. It is called *La Valse (The Waltz)* by Camille Claudel. I say the words to myself again and again, *La Valse, The Waltz,* because there is a sway to them like dancing. The sculpture is a man and a woman entwined. They are stone-still, caught in a moment, but they seem to be constantly moving. The woman's falling-off dress floats out from her in billowing folds, and it makes me think of our Christmas angels, though there is something so much more radiant here. A beauty so unsettling I cannot look at it for long.

Every morning I look out into the street through the tiny window. Here there are no chipmunks. There are a million big black squirrels and precious few small red ones. The pigeons step right into our path on the sidewalk, jutting purple-blue velvet heads. Their red feet frightening like an organ exposed. Pigeons make up most of the birds here, whereas at home there are grosbeaks, blue jays, chickadees, whippoorwills, woodpeckers, swallows, and hummingbirds, the tiniest of all. This is what's missing here—the birds and the butterflies. Perhaps there is no room for them, for truly it seems that every space is occupied by someone or something. Uncle William would be glum to know it. Everywhere Lucy takes us I look for them, but they are few and far between. On the wide sidewalk of Yonge Street I look to the pavement for caterpillars and find crushed cigarettes. Dirt settles into the foam of our flip-flops.

"This is the longest street in the world," Lucy tells us. She squeezes my shoulder.

It's something, to be the longest, I can hear it in her voice. At home, next to Townline Road, which has only trees and creeks with tadpoles, the longest street is Ridge Road. It runs right through downtown, past the Whistle Stop, past the bank and the chip truck, and up the hill to the highway, which cuts across its top. Yonge Street, old street, goes on forever, no street stops it. Stores scream loud music and flash neon signs and people push by or stand in the way in impenetrable groups. I hear pieces of conversations—"grab a coffee" and "hilarious!" and "no point crying"—and I try to string them together, sing them into something. Foreign speech like music jingles in my ears. Rolling Italian, xylophone Chinese. Here people come from everywhere. In shades of pink and brown, some so black there is purple in them. At home, with the odd exotic exception, people come in white only. Peachy pink, the colour of me, of you, of paper dolls. Our Hallowe'en twins were almost that colour, formed from papier mâché. Those twins were at home still, in the closet. Some of our clothes there too, maybe ripped up, maybe just waiting to be on us again.

I look down at my greying flip-flops. The streets are dirty. There are garbage cans on every corner, but there is garbage in between too, sometimes lifted by wind and flying. When I say so, complaining, Lucy calls me crazy.

"Toronto might just be the cleanest city in the world," she says.

But at night the garbagemen take the sacks of garbage from the cans and dump the contents and put the dirty sacks back in, I have seen it happen. With a shovel they spread the garbage around in the back of the truck and a sour smell rises up from there. Back home, Wednesday is garbage day. Two men come by in a yellow-and-white truck, one driving, one riding on the back, and they take away the tidy Glad bags each with its twist tie in place.

We come from a spotless town, but I have not known another. The water rushing by is a river that washes the air. Here there is no such thing. There is a lake, we have seen it on the map, but I cannot see it anywhere, no matter where I go. There is no smell of it in the air, nor a layer of moisture on my skin. And on the unwashed streets people sit. They turn their grimy hats up like bowls and collect shining coins in them. Lucy says we shouldn't stare but the street people do, holding us with their weird eyes, the whites too white in their dirty faces. An old woman sits on a grubby blanket, too hot for the hot day, arms folded, fingers pulling at the long grey hairs of her underarms. She smiles black teeth at me and then at you, and we move away from her, below ground in a herd of strangers, following the arrows to a subterranean world. Lucy speaks to the man in the booth through a hole in the glass. He looks blankly at her, not smiling, and out spill the tokens, fake dimes, lightweight. She scoops them up and gives us each one, slowing the line, causing shoving and aggravation. I put the fake money in the slot and push against the turnstile. It moves so easily, as though I've tricked it, an outsider sneaking in. And we stand on the long platform with the crowd, looking across like into a mirror. Even down here there are too many people. We can never get away from them. Most of them rushing, unhappy, travelling alone. On either end of the platform is a black hole, who knows where it takes us? Down in the tracks I see a mouse flit, maybe a rat. Something lives everywhere, in all the corners. Living underground, travelling underground, roofs pressing down.

The noise comes first, not like a real train. And then it bursts through the hole, long and dull silver, causing wind that stops our breath, moving too fast to stop but stopping anyway, everyone rushing towards it. Lucy gripping my elbow, pushing me through. Where are you? My heart flutters strangely, a butterfly in there. Could we get caught in the doors?

Into my hair Lucy whispers, "Soon it will be old hat," and I see the old hats, bowls, the empty people with shining eyes. Getting on and off doesn't seem like something I will ever do calmly, but here I am, you across from me, hurtling through the tunnel, windows of blackness whipping by showing constantly my own reflection. A stranger beside me on the sticky orange seat. Here, everywhere we go we get on something that will take us there faster.

You press your face against the glass, fogging the window and picking up germs. Invisible germs of strangers crawl everywhere. Germs are alive, like people. Here they are teeming. On the seat beneath. On the rubber escalator strip we laid our hands on. I can feel them moving from the stranger beside me onto my own skin.

Later I feel them again, above ground in daylight. We are shopping for dinner. In Toronto you can buy vegetables not just in stores but right on the street. I choose the tomatoes, checking for fingernail breaks in the skins. Mrs. Livingston at home pressed her long thumbnail into fruit and vegetables to test the juiciness. Does Dad know to watch for that? Here we don't know who has touched the food before us or how many strange hands have been there.

And how many hands have been here, at Goodwill, the sorriest place in the world? We are shopping, buying up the dirty cast-offs of others. I run my hands along the backs of couches, which smell of bodies, and you sprawl on those couches, not caring. How can you, Eugenie? Sometimes you are just like me and sometimes you are just the opposite. Lucy buys used pots and pans, chipped plates. Also a used curling iron to curl her straight bright hair, and in the brush are foreign black strands and flakes of scalp.

"I'll wash it!" she says, pooh-poohing my disgusted look.

Even you are disgusted. You who will eat what you've dropped on the floor, just blowing to set the germs free.

Then in our home below ground I wipe my face with a cloth that came from our other home. I wash my hands and city grime spirals down the drain. I look long at my other self in the mirror, where a cockroach, a roach, rests on the glass. At night I sink into bed and look at the tiny window, waiting for the ghost, which you have not since mentioned. I don't ask, because I don't want to know, but every night I try to sense its presence. All I can feel is you and me, and further off, Lucy. But if something is here, I am ready. You sleep soundly beside me.

How had I come here? There was the subway, that man, and then a hole in my memory, and I stood on the long glitzy platform at Bloor and Yonge, where once a crazy man pushed a girl to her death.

Was that now or back then?

I looked down at my legs in their snug black tights, my plaid jacket, my whole self like a stranger's outfit pulled on. Those boots on my feet, they were scuffed. I told myself to think of where I got them and when, pull myself back, or forward. Vancouver—Simon sneering at their impracticality. Pointing out the thin leather, which would crack in the cold. Ankle-high with zippers and wafer soles, I could feel the chill through them. Not boots but glass slippers, Simon said.

"They're ridiculous. They'll never get you through the winter."

"What do you know about winter?" I scoffed. "Vancouver has no winter—I'm from Ontario, remember?"

"Then why don't you know how to dress for the cold? Those boots," he said, "are made for ballroom dancing."

"Then take me," I said, and right there on the street he held my hand and placed his arm on my waist and whisked me around in widening circles.

Where was he with his smart remarks and common sense? If he were here right now, I'd rub my neck against his neck. Whose skin was that, so smooth? I'd hold my eye right close to his eye so our lashes touched, our pupils blurred. And then tell him: *Simon, I had a twin.*

To fill time I walked along Bloor Street. I stared at the debris that filled the cracks in the sidewalks. Crumbled leaves, city dirt. Human hair and flakes of skin and peeled fingernails. Fragments of so many people.

CHAPTER 8 **REFLECTION**

The story of Ildikoh had come to me while playing Scrabble with Simon. Just like you, he couldn't spell well, Eugenie, but he played the game strategically and often won. I chose words for their whimsy rather than for how many points they might give. We couldn't talk while we played because Simon had to concentrate, it was understandable. He was always hoping for that turn where he'd use all of his letters. Scrabble didn't work that way for me. Instead it was like Alphaghetti, letters making words making stories.

As Simon pondered his options, I waited and stared at the board. *Meander* then *linger*. *Woe* then *groom*. *Horn* then *face*.

Ildikoh, she walked alone. But, the further she went from him, the more she longed to meander back to him. Did he not see what they had? Did he not care? By the ocean she lingered, looking into the waves. Something in his dreams had drawn him to water again and again, and she had gone with him, walked sleepily beside him. Now at her toe was a snail wedged in sand. She bent and scooped him up, that snail, and peered inside at his moist grey body. In her travels she had seen snails make love. They rose lazily out of their shells and pressed soft against soft, no skin to distance them, no mask, only flesh against flesh. Woe she would be without Hal, her groom. His missing horn no longer spiralled like the shell of this lone snail. His face no longer pressed so close to hers.

"Your turn," said Simon.

I placed my tiles on the board. *Daft*. Good word.

That Stephen, he was daft. Spelling his name with a *p-h* instead of a *v*, then calling himself Hal. Wearing a hat all those years. Leading her on. But how to fall out of love when she was so deeply in it? Would that love sat in a glass and she could pour it out into the ocean once it spoiled, love being a perishable good. A good gone bad. Would that she could remove love from her soul the way she had removed her seeing-eye horn, the way that surgeon had removed Hal's horn, rendering him Stephen. What else had been taken from him that fateful day? Or had she seen something in Hal that had never been there, a hallucination of sorts, a version of him that existed only in her own imagination? She had seen her mirror image in his horn, even with the hat to cover it. Woe was she now that it was gone.

Lucy had that smooth circle scar on her forehead, remember? She tells us a horn had once grown there, that she had been a unicorn in another life, that in a way she still is that unicorn and always will be. She says nothing, no one, is ever truly extinct.

"Even dodo birds?" you say, smirking.

"Well, yes," she says. "Even dodo birds. Look at Daddy!"

Simon laughed upon winning the game.

"Imagine!" he said with mock humility. "You, Miss Spelling Bee, losing to me!"

For I had told him about the interminable spelling bees in which Rebecca and I were the only two left standing. It was a safe story—it didn't give away anything about you or Lucy or Dad.

Now I could see his spelling mistakes glowing on the board. *Cul. Ragu.* I had not noticed them during the game, had skimmed over them in search of inspiration from the prettier words. Simon was no winner of spelling bees, but there was the chance he had purposely cheated, knowing it should be *cull, ragout,* but believing anything went in Scrabble.

"It's not ragu," I said, pointing to the error. "Ragu is spaghetti sauce in a jar, it has a capital. The real ragout should be o-u-t."

Simon laughed. *"The real ragout,"* he mimicked. "You mean they spelled it wrong on the jar?"

I smiled and kissed him.

"You cheated," I said.

"I won," he said.

That was before. That was when he hoped he'd found in me his other half.

"Maybe we were separated at birth," he told me. "Whatever I can't do, you can, and vice versa. I can cook ragout and you can't. You can spell *ragout* and I can't."

All I did was roll my eyes. I told him he could use the dictionary when we played, I wouldn't mind, but always he said this: "How can you look up a word in the dictionary when you don't know how to spell it?" It made me feel cold because that was what you would say, Eugenie. You who wrote *well* for *will*.

How well you know.

It changed the meaning of things.

We play Scrabble in the clementine room of our underground city home. Outside is a frosty swath of oak leaves pressed against the too-small basement window, so this is fall, nearly winter. Slit of cold air spilling in through the crack between door and floor.

Poor you, Eugenie, you can't spell worth beans, so the game takes forever, and when finally you lay your tiles on the board, you lay them crookedly, sometimes upside down, and I straighten and turn them, because how can you concentrate with them every which way?

Sometimes I lean over and make a word for you. On your pew is an *R* on its side, an *M* like a *W*. That must be how you see things, even right-side up. That disarrayed way. You with your smart mixed-up brain.

"You could make *roam*," I tell you. "Or *moan*."

You pause to look at your letters, and then at me. "What else?" you ask.

"*Morn. Main.* If it didn't have a capital you could make *Maori*."

"Does it *have* to have a capital?"

"Well, it should."

"But does it *have* to?"

"Yes. According to the rules."

"But *all* the letters are capitals!" You hold one up to show me, as if I don't know. "Why do they make them capitals if you aren't even allowed to use capitals?"

"Do you have an *E*?"

You pause again and look. "No. Why?"

"If you did, you could make *marine*. That's a nice one, don't you think?"

You sit looking at your letters and then you look up at me, smirking. "Do *you* have an *E*?"

Just now a gust of cold air and in comes Lucy in her second-hand outfit, a jacket too short in the sleeves. With her comes an oak leaf, scuttling dry across the floor. Home from her art class, so Wednesday night. This week a new painting of shiny apples and bottles with squares of light on them.

"It's a still life," she tells us.

"What's that?" you ask, pointing to the white square.

"Light," she says. "Reflection."

Together we look at it. You press your finger on it, blotting it out. The square is like a tiny label, a blank, a mistake.

"It's good," you tell her.

She hangs the paintings up around the apartment, each week a new one, always of fruit and bottles or flowers in a vase. At first they make her happy, we can see that by the flush of her cheeks, the breathlessness when she rushes in to show us. For us, it is this more than anything else that makes the paintings beautiful.

Wednesday nights we are not to answer the phone. It might be him calling, and if he knew she had left us alone, he would turn ugly. Other kids are left alone at ten, we know, and Lucy knows too. Rebecca and even Evie, whose parents are religious, were allowed to go any-where they wanted from age eight on. But not us. Not here especially. Not ever, if he had his way. Lucy does not believe it is wrong to leave us. She trusts us more with ourselves than with strangers, she says. She waits outside, looking in the window while we bolt and chain the locks, and then we move to the front window to watch her go. We are full of pride for her, our mother in someone else's colourful clothes. Swinging her long arms as she walks to catch the streetcar. Smiling and waving goodbye.

We are unafraid. No one can get us here. We are in our own secret cocoon.

And yet there is a chill one Wednesday when the phone rings. The shrill of it is shocking and we sit with the Scrabble board between us, just looking at each other. It rings twelve times and then it stops and starts again. Each time, twelve times. Poor him, he is counting. Tonight he's got nothing to do. It feels wrong not to answer, like lying. The way it keeps ringing might mean he knows we are here. I can see his sad face in my mind as though he is right in front of me, not a million miles away.

We try to keep playing. You put down this word, *candie,* which is wrong but I let you. The *I* and the *E* are more a sign of thinking than not. But with my turn the phone starts again and I cannot make any sense of my letters because I am counting too, all the way to twelve, that's how well I know him. I would like to hear his voice, the kind one, saying hello in my ear. I reach my hand out and place it on the receiver but your hand reaches too, pressing mine down. I can feel the ringing in my palm, up my arm to the shoulder.

"Don't," you say.

"He'll just keep calling and calling."

"And what do you think he'll say if Lucy's not here?"

That was something.

"We could lie," I say. "We could tell him she's having a bath."

You just roll your eyes. "You can't lie worth beans," you say, which is true, I cannot, I never could lie worth beans, though later I will learn.

The phone stops and then starts again. I look at you.

"*You* could lie," I say.

"No," you tell me. "I'm not answering."

So we sit and we play and all the while I think of him in his frayed brown chair, the phone in his lap. Maybe Blue on the floor beside him. Too far from us and lonely, wondering only why we do not answer and how is it that we can bear to be away? If I could, I would send him a telepathic message, saying simply that I miss him, that I love him, that I wish to be home.

How is it that you do not, Eugenie?

When Lucy comes in the phone is ringing again and the sound of that washes the smile from her face. She looks at you and at me. She lets the painting slide to the floor and she answers.

"Hello?"

The ease with which she will lie to our father is astounding.

"Oh, out and about."

Her painting is of bruiseless apples, red and green.

"To the library and then to the park."

You touch your finger to a place that's still wet and then look at the colour on your skin.

I think he must know we are lying because why would we go to the park on a fall night that is cold and windy? He must not ask, not wanting to know, since next all she says to him is, "Mm-hmm, really fun."

I am watching you, I want to catch your eye, but you do not look up from Lucy's painting. The squares that represent reflection are taking on a truer appearance. It may mean she is learning, though she has always said art is more than duplication, what, we do not know.

Now she is pointing to us and to the receiver, meaning do we want to say hello, which we do not, not now, and we shake our heads in unison.

Too smoothly she says, "They're just in brushing their teeth and getting ready for bed. Can you call back tomorrow night?"

I feel dirty and sick, not saying hello. But in the midst of such deception I know I could not stand to hear his voice, especially the kind one, or to trade those goodbye lines with him: *See ya later, Alligator. In a while, Crocodile.*

Instead, before bed I write a letter, and my guilt is only assuaged the next morning, when I slide it into the dark mouth of the mailbox and know it's on its way to him.

Dear Daddy,

How are you? I am fine. In school we are learning about different kinds of clouds, which ones mean rain and which ones don't. Cirrus are the ones that look like feathers. Cumulus are the fat wool-ball ones that are flat on the bottom and come in a very bright shade of white. Nimbus are white plus grey because they have rain in them. Sometimes the nimbus clouds are so big they cover the whole sky so they don't look like a cloud any more, just a grey day, but that is what it really is when it is grey out, a nimbus cloud. We are also learning how to speak French. I can say a lot of French words like comment ça va, which is how are you and bon jour. It means good day but it really means Hello because that is more the way we say it in English. This week is Halloween but it is not very cold here yet. I am going as a Senorita because Lucy has a red skirt with a pink skirt inside it and I have those clackers you clack with your hands from that time Miss Reese went to Spain. Eugenie wants to be a rainbow but we don't know how to make it yet. Will you please pet Blue for me?

Love, Janie.

It is after this that it snows and snows. White covers the tiny window, blocking our only view. The ants and earwigs stop emerging from the baseboards but the cockroaches stay. You race to the bathroom, flip the light on to see them scurry. "A bug is a bug," you say, but I disagree, they disgust me.

Those people who live on the street, they disgust me too. Many will die this winter, it happens every year. They don't want to sleep in the shelters, so at night the police drive around and lock them up like jailbirds, maybe in striped pyjamas, it's for their own good. How is it they can be so cold as to die? I can see my breath, true, but it's not as cold here as at home, our other home, where the snowbanks are castles, where once a boy died in a snow-fort tunnel. And here there are warm places to go: shopping malls, the long narrow world underground. Places made for them. Missions with long rows of lined-up beds, hot food to eat. Vents in the sidewalks give off gusts of warm air, I've felt that myself.

But Lucy's heart swells for the weird-eyes. Her own jacket is too small, long monkey arms swinging out as she walks, flash of skinny wrist exposed above each pink mitten, and still she presses quarters into the hands of strangers, their fingers yellow from nicotine. Some days she gives away all of our lightweight tokens, all of our change, and we have to walk to where we're going, snot-wet scarves tied tight against our faces, skin chapped from cold.

Today she has on green plaid bell-bottoms, clashing with the patched coat and pink mittens, and shame heats my face. She is weird, weird, weird, he is right. I'd like to be with him now, at home with you, with our fake Siamese twins, in our bunk-bed room, just reading and lying with Blue. I miss Blue. I miss the cool wet of his nose on my skin, do you? The cracked pads of his paws, which smell in a way like toe jam. I do not want to be here, on slushy streets where the snow is brown and inedible. But you, Eugenie, I think you do.

We walk and walk. There is a weird-eye in a phone booth, her open hand sticking out through the doors. She is barely visible through the frosty glass, but from the knees down we have a clear view. Masking tape around her shoe to keep it from flapping open like a flapping mouth but still her toe slides out, the toenail thick and yellow with ridgy lines all over. The skin hard and scaly, blue from the cold. Lucy is watching the weird-eye through the crack in the door, smiling sorry, no change, and though we pass I know we will not get far. I can read Lucy's face. White and tight in the cold, eyes shifting, it tells me she cannot not help.

"No," I say when Lucy stops. "Please, let's not go back."

Walking in the snow in heavy boots, my legs like lead, I'm exhausted.

"Okay, okay," Lucy says, but I know she does not mean it. We walk some more, and we are blocks away when she stops at a coffee shop and breaks the twenty-dollar bill that is for groceries, for hot delicious soup and fingers of toast with margarine. She buys the weird-eye steaming coffee, me moaning, "Nooo, it's too cold to go back."

Lucy pauses, holding the lid in her hand. Her humiliating mittens dangle like a child's mittens, from strings that disappear into her sleeves. She looks into the cup. "Do you think she takes cream? Sugar?"

"Both," you say. "She needs lots of both." And you stir them in and fasten the lid and carry the cup and it shocks me how separate we are.

We move back down the street in the cold, blocks and blocks, undoing all the progress we've made. We are like a warm blanket unravelling into nothing but a useless tangled mass of wool. My own feet are numb though there are no holes in my boots, but I do not have room in me to think of how freezing the weird-eyes must be. Beyond feeling, perhaps.

That woman, she's still there, her hand stuck out, asking for something. You hand me the cup and push me forward, and though I don't want to go closer, she's seen me, is waiting. I peer into the crack and look into the woman's weird eyes, less weird close up. Is she crazy? I hold out the cup, which by now is cold and squashed, coffee dirtying the white lid and dripping down the white sides. The woman smiles, pushes her face through the crack in the doors. She squeezes her dirty hands around the cup and lets out a long sigh, which clouds the air and smells of food gone bad.

"God bless," she says.

I dream of her black teeth smiling. Of her laugh full of phlegm and her hand reaching out to get me. Cars and people rush by, but unseen she pulls me into her phone-booth house and I am searching for you through the dirty glass. All I can see is white snow falling so fast, so thick, that everything turns invisible. The people and the cars and the buildings, sky-high. The deluge of shapes and colours becomes a monochrome wash of white. The lady is laughing in my ears and I push against the doors but she grabs my hair and pulls me back. I stomp on her foot with my boot and push again at the doors, and just as she howls I fly through and land in a snow-dome world. The flakes fall without sound. Oh, it is so quiet. No one is anywhere here.

And now I am awake with the dream still in me. From bright white to black I go. I lie in the darkness and feel for the ghost, but feel nothing.

CHAPTER 9 IN SYNCHRONY

I had walked all day, and when I returned I discovered my luggage had arrived. Dolores lifted the bag, put it on the counter between us and smiled at me. She had a missing tooth and the others were yellow. When I reached for my bag she grabbed my hand in hers and squeezed.

"If you wanna stay," she said, locking eyes with me, "stay."

I was so stunned that I simply stood there, staring at her. I had the sickly feeling she'd gone through all my things with her stained yellow fingers. That I would smell her on my clothes when I opened my luggage. And yet there was hardly anything to be learned of me that way. The little books would be puzzling, she might be unable to read between the lines. Other than them, the bag held nothing of great consequence, despite the fact that nearly all I had left was inside it.

I climbed the stairs to my room and sat a long time on the edge of the bed. I took the books out of my bag and laid each one on the floor in front of me. I thought of how you would have admired Simon's covers, how Lucy would too. I had never shown her, never even told her of the books, but I knew she knew. After each one was published, she wrote a letter of congratulations. She even thanked me. She said they were a joy to read. Only once did I respond. I said in all honesty that I should be thanking her for all the stories she had told me as a child. *Us*, though that I did not say. I told her that I loved her, that I hoped she always knew. And afterwards I was so drained that for three days I could barely get out of bed.

"What's wrong?" Simon asked.

"Flu," I said, missing a perfect moment for revelation.

But writing to Lucy had upset me so much that I couldn't conceive of telling him the whole story from beginning to end. From then on I sent a card at Christmas, signing "Jane" beneath a message printed for the masses.

Now, in the motel room, I lifted the receiver and hung it up again. I did that three times before calling. On the other end the phone rang and rang, and then my father answered.

"I'm still coming," I said. "It's just that my luggage—they don't know where it is. But I'm coming. I'll be there soon."

Again I ran a bath in the gritty tub and let the hot water sting me. I thought, Maybe I am partly crazy. I felt less and less present, more and more like air, as though only my body existed here and the real me was somewhere else, in limbo. I put my feet on the taps, the left on the hot and the right on the cold. I could easily turn the left tap with my foot, but not the right. Simon always said that I was so left-handed I was actually left-sided. Once he saw a program about twins and discovered that a great many of them were left-handed. There was even some extreme theory, he said, that all single-born left-handers had originally been twins whose other half had early on been washed from the womb.

"Come and watch this," he kept calling from the living room, but I stayed in my study. "You've got to see this!" he called.

If ever there had been a time to tell him, that was it. Instead I wrote a story.

PIROUETTE

When the baby was still growing inside her, Etoile felt sure there were two babies because of the constant turning, turning in the womb. To Henri, she said, "I think we have twins," and she placed his large archeologist's hand on her oh-so-large belly that he too might feel the double tumbling there. Even when the doctor said no, there is only one heartbeat, Etoile believed the two tiny hearts were merely beating in mischievous unison.

The months passed and the babies grew larger inside Etoile, each growing eyes and a nose—first the nostrils, black holes in a flat face, and then the nose itself, protruding. Etoile was gladdened to think of them breathing, though she didn't understand it. How could the little ones get air, sealed as they were in her black watery womb? This Etoile could not ponder for long without panic engulfing her, and so she focused instead on the fact that, yes, the babies grew larger and stronger each day, as evidenced by Etoile's own burgeoning girth. By now they had fingers and toes, which Etoile could feel drumming against the taut skin of her stomach, an inverted bongo. Their hearts drummed in tandem between the spaces of Etoile's heartbeat, creating surprising rhythm.

"Any day now," said Etoile to Henri.

They were beaming. They had the bright hopeful faces of parents-to-be.

But oh, *quelle surprise* when a single tiny baby emerged!

Etoile pushed again and waited.

"C'est tout," said the doctor.

Etoile lifted her head and looked at the newborn child, a girl. She put her hand on her stomach but there was no heartbeat there, nothing left inside except the workings of her own emptied body. Etoile was stunned.

"Where is the other?" she asked the doctor.

"Other? There is no other. I told you before, Madame. This baby is your one and only."

Etoile looked again at the child. The only far-fetched sign of the missing twin showed in the baby's strange feet—two left and no right, an unfathomable mix-up!

Etoile and Henri counted the toes, which rightly numbered ten, though ordered wrongly, and they looked down upon them, all unsmiling. This was not what they'd expected. The baby, too, was unsmiling, and though Etoile knew babies didn't smile right away—who would when thrust into a glaring, foreign world?—this baby seemed particularly aloof. And something else was wrong. She did not have the smooth baby skin of one newly born, but skin that was rough and dry, as though made from sandpaper. Until she looked into the baby's gentle eyes, one blue, one green, Etoile felt almost as though it were raining (for she was allergic to rain). A horrible rage bubbled within and curiously dissipated as her eyes met those of her baby.

It hurt to hold her, yet they did so. Her baby skin scratched their arms and scraped their kissing faces. Grief filled all of huge Henri, and also Etoile, beginning in the empty black womb and working up, up and out through her now-crying eyes. A tear landed on the baby's flaking forehead and a smooth moist circle of pink appeared and quickly dried again.

She was a wee thing. Small like a doll, and bony. Etoile and Henri were astonished that their overwhelming love had created such an underwhelming specimen. Such a frail and tiny creature. For Henri, he was larger than life, and Etoile, though petite in stature, was full and round, substantial. If babies were brought by the long beaks of storks, it would be reasonable. But babies were not, and so it was incongruous.

Still, they fell in love with her. They swooned in her singular presence.

Cuddling in bed with their strange baby between them, Etoile whispered, "She's bound to be special."

"Mais oui," Henri replied. *"Certainement."*

They named her Pirouette, recalling how she had tumbled so wildly in the womb. As it turned out, the name was doubly appropriate, for when she first learned to walk, Pirouette went always in circles, owing to her two left feet.

People laughed, as people will.

"Pirouette!" they tittered. "The girl who walks in circles!"

"Never mind," Etoile and Henri told themselves and each other. "Never mind," they told Pirouette.

Nightly, when they tucked her in and placed moist soothing kisses on her chafed cheek, they recounted the story of their wedding, which had been out of doors, at night, under the stars. A bruised sky had threatened to rain down on them all day long, and Etoile, who abhorred the rain, had been ready to leave Henri at the altar, believing the clouds a bad omen. They stood in the courtyard, she at one end, he at the other. Sensing her mood, and knowing it to be volatile, everyone waited to see what she would do. The moonflowers opened their bright white faces and out from their sun-shy centres came the sweetest of fragrances. A perfumed brightness shone from the vines. Etoile looked at Henri, who grinned and pointed to the sky. She looked up. A patch of stars had appeared directly above her. When the rain began, it soaked everyone but the bride and groom. Such weddings, they were told, produced unions whose children would change the world dramatically.

But as she grew, which she did oh so slowly, Pirouette seemed far from dramatic. Rather she seemed dry and plain, not the way to be when you were Parisian.

"*C'est bizarre,*" said Etoile.

"*C'est la vie,*" said Henri.

Even Etoile's best friend Babette said, "*C'est dommage,*" tut-tutting.

Babette had a child of her own, a boy named Leo, who had green eyes that were disturbingly becoming, and *café-au-lait* skin and a huge red afro. He was anything but plain. When she brought him to Etoile's house and placed him next to Pirouette, *pauvre* Pirouette almost disappeared beside him, so eclipsing was his presence. So vibrant was he. So plain and dry was she.

And they sat and stared blankly at each other.

When they were old enough to speak, he asked her, "What's the matter with you?"

Pirouette thought. An answer floated out, but she did not know where it came from. "I am only half of myself," she said.

Leo looked puzzled. He knitted his coppery brows.

"Oh," he said.

They grew up side by side, Leo growing creamier and lovelier day by day, laughing brightly and smiling with lips that were full and soft, unchappable. It was he who taught Pirouette to walk in a straight line. Or rather, because of him, she taught herself.

One day he mused dreamily, "Sometimes I wish we could just go and keep going and then come back again." She didn't understand the point of such a boomerang journey, but so fiercely did she love him that she longed to go where he went, to follow him everywhere. It was not that she couldn't get to the places she wanted to get to in her own circular way. It was just that it took longer. She had to change the size and the shape of her circles in order to achieve a journey that was less immediately circuitous. Whereas Leo simply put one foot in front of the other and went where he wanted to go in a straight line, his afro bobbing. And it was willpower—the will to be near him and the unswerving power of her steps—that helped Pirouette do the same.

The little buskins helped too. Henri this year had given her the ancient booties as a birthday present. He told her they had come from a dig in Athens, the birthplace of tragedy, and that they had surely been worn by a tiny two-left-feet tragedian. This she did not question. Someone just like me, she thought, pulling the time-worn boots over her rough sockless feet. (Sockless because you try wearing something knitted on skin as dry as hers!)

Once she was on the straight and narrow, everyone forgot about her strange affliction. Well, that one, anyway. Two well-behaved left feet you could hide easily enough in boots that were albeit strange, so rounded were the toes. But a dryness as severe as Pirouette's could not be masked. Now it was this that people tittered about. Instead of poking fun at her feet, they poked fun at her skin, which was rough and dusty. Behind her back and sometimes to her face they scoffed about how they should not speak in breathy voices or laugh their gusting laughs too close lest Pirouette crumple and disperse into the air. As though she were a leaf dryly falling.

Yes, she was that dry.

And plain.

As Babette liked to point out. Babette, who, when Leo was a baby, they could see coming from blocks away. He rode on her back, like a papoose, and his red afro frizzed out behind her so that, from a distance, it seemed like her afro. Which was hilarious, of course, because Babette was un-afro-like and expertly groomed. The only time she had appeared remotely ungroomed in public had been at Etoile and Henri's wedding. And that had been out of her control. What could you do if a rogue cloud burst open above you and soaked you right through, down to your specially dyed shoes? Before then and since then, Babette was immaculately turned out. To Pirouette, she seemed just like a movie star, with her smooth skin stretched over high cheekbones, a faint glow of rouge there. She wore a lipstick called *L'amour mauve*, it said so on the bottom of the tube, and the fragrance from that mixed with her own mysterious fragrance, which was fruity but not, flowery but not. Pirouette loved the smell. It lingered on Leo, on his skin and in his hair, just from being near her.

Pirouette tried forever to place the fragrance, sniffing narcissi and tiny sweet muscari that pushed through the tough spring soil. In the summer, smelling bubblegum snapdragons with their snapping dragon mouths. Smelling the fruit on the trees and even the more exotic ones in the juices she drank. And there were many juices—almost too many to count. Her extraordinary dryness brought about an extreme unquenchable thirst, and each day she guzzled seven glasses of guava juice, nine glasses of passion-fruit punch, four glasses of youngberry juice, four glasses of elderberry juice and eleven glasses of mango juice, her undeniable favourite. The juice as it touched her lips disappeared from the glass. And still she'd be thirsty! To Etoile she'd plead, "*S'il-vous-plait, Maman,* may I have some more?"

And her mother would say, *"Zut alors!"* and pour that juice, because truly Pirouette was small and thin and dry, dry, dry.

She had brittle fingernails and toenails that snapped off as soon as the white parts showed. She had brittle brown hair riddled with split ends. If she tried to grow it past her earlobes, it only broke off and looked jagged and unflattering. And her skin she wore like a layer of white dust. If she blew on her arm or leg or belly, a gust of loose powder rose into the air and then settled again.

Though she drew all liquid to her, still her thirst could not be quenched. Which was a great pity, because how she loved to be out of doors, searching for the source of Babette's smell and feeling the breeze and watching the spanned wings of birds rising. And yet her very presence there turned green grass brown. When she walked with Leo in the garden, following his perfect footprints, the damp soil dried to a sandy crumble beneath her oddly matching feet. When she fingered the moist petals of flowers or the fine points of leaves, they dried to crisp parchment at her touch. Her favourite flower was the hydrangea, because it was as thirsty as she was. Its name was Greek for water vessel, and its blooms were as appealing dry as they were fresh . . . well, almost.

One summer afternoon she was walking with Leo in the Jardin des Plantes, where there was a little zoo and also a whole school devoted solely to the study of plants and flowers. She was following his straight line between the huge and ancient trees when she saw a ladybug alight on his shoulder. She watched the lady for a long time, riding there, and when she saw her lift her spotty umbrella wings and hover towards Pirouette, she smiled. She put her arm out in welcome, knowing instinctively that ladybugs are rarely afraid. When the ladybug landed, a white puff of dust rose from Pirouette's bare dry arm, and the lady coughed and sputtered.

"Sorry," whispered Pirouette.

The little lady looked up and smiled warmly, but she seemed unwell. She coughed again and lifted once more her strange shell wings, and Pirouette heard them cracking. All her spots, they slid off as the lady flew away, and an army of ants carried them home for feasting. Pirouette touched the place on her arm where the lady had been, a smooth oasis drying. She would have cried if she could have, but her ducts were both tearless.

And then her dismay was entirely forgotten, for Leo turned to face her, grinning widely and standing stalk-still. A butterfly rested on his frizz of red hair. Pirouette stood watching with her mouth fallen open. The butterfly was large and iridescent. So many colours shimmered on its wings that it could not have been called one colour. She knew that scales of colour covered those wings, like the scales of a fish but fine as powder. Beneath the scales its wings were transparent, and that was amazing, to think that butterflies might be fluttering see-through in the air.

Leo reached his hand to his hair and the butterfly stepped gracefully onto his finger with her long thin legs, like a lady holding up the skirt of her ballgown. He held the creature out to Pirouette. Over-large and splendid, it began to pulsate with some special life force. Entranced, enchanted, not thinking, Pirouette stretched out her arm to meet Leo's, the tips of her dusty white fingers touching the tips of his supple brown ones.

Magically, the butterfly climbed on and rested on the desert of Pirouette for one breathtaking moment, until scale by scale all its beauty fell away and it flew off, silently see-through but for its sleek black body. Pirouette cried tearless tears, invisible too. But that was not the last thing in a heart-breaking day.

Leo took her to the edge of the Seine. He hoped it might help her feel happy, to be near water. They sat counting the *bateaux mouches* that floated to and from the Tour Eiffel, and by the time Leo showed her the snail that had climbed onto his bare brown knee, Pirouette had forgotten the spotless lady and the see-through butterfly.

Leo made a joke: "S. Cargo, he's called, because everywhere he goes he takes his cargo with him," and Pirouette laughed because, though his jokes inevitably emerged in the shape of chestnuts, she still found everything he said delightful.

The snail was delightful too, with his suit and his suitable name. He had a squishy little head and his ears, which were not ears but eyes, wiggled and poked at the sky. Never thinking, only feeling, she let him climb on. He stretched further out of his shell and pressed his body onto her arm. Her dryness drew so much of his wetness from him that he could no longer stick to her skin, and S. Cargo tucked his head back into his shell and then fell in his spiral way to the ground. He was lucky, she thought, that he could protect himself from her.

They looked at S. lying there and then they looked blankly at each other. Leo's green eyes deepened and filled with the salt water she could not know. She wished she had a shell exterior. A little house she could hide in when things went wrong. And it was then that she decided: She would stop going outside altogether, for what was the point in joy if it always held hands with sorrow?

And so her life grew small. Less dramatic, even, than it had been. Like S., she poked her head out now and again through her bedroom window, but her house, it stayed firmly around her. She was never exhilarated, but she was not despondent either. She had achieved a kind of balance. In her soul she was flat, like the rubber doll she'd once owned, who disappeared in profile except for her plume of yellow hair, which, anyway, Pirouette did not have.

Leo came daily. He told her of all he saw and touched, and through him she lived vicariously. He smelled of the fresh outside, and she breathed him in, listening to his tumble of stories about bees and the many-eyed dragonfly and a pigeon who was pure white, even his beak and feet. He brought her a feather as proof and he tickled her rough face with that softness.

Every time he left she drank umpteen glasses of juice, thirstier than usual, and then soaked in the tub, though the water evaporated so quickly it was hardly worth it to bathe at all. Hardly necessary either. Dirt didn't stick to Pirouette. It fell right off, like sand from skin that has not been swimming.

Ah, swimming, she thought. It might be what she missed most in her new life as a recluse. So badly did she long to swim that she dreamed herself one in a long line of girls wearing tutus and dancing in a turquoise pool. Pirouette could see all of them mirrored when she looked up at the roof of water. They moved in synchrony, Pirouette and the others pirouetting and pliéing, and the incredible tutus held their shape, staying dry to the touch by some magical repulsion of the water they were immersed in. Pirouette laid her hands on the stiff skirt as she danced. She watched the mingled bubbles of breath, hers and the other dancers', and she wondered how it was possible to breathe underwater without gills or a tank on your back.

She thought there must be magic in this water, that that was what made it too blue. So content was she, she was not aware of being unthirsty. Until that thought, the pin in a balloon. For when you are dreaming you are really just watching yourself. Unhappily, there are always two of you. And this dreamer was as thirsty, as dry, as ever.

She woke to the sound of heavy rain. She smelled the water in the air and was filled with the double pull of pleasure and dismay, loving that fragrant freshness and the wet air and the brightened glow of all moistened things against the flat dull grey of dawn. When it rained, she felt her heart expand, and her lungs, briefly fat and pink, were cleared of all the dusty debris she had wheezed into herself.

And yet there was also Etoile. Already Pirouette heard her wailing. When it rained, Etoile spiralled into madness. It had something to do with the barometric pressure. Alternately moaning and shrieking, she pulled at her hair. A toe that had once been bitten by frost swelled and purpled like an old drunk's nose. Pirouette dreaded the sight of that throbbing discoloured digit. The toe meant a masquerader had replaced her mother. The masquerader would release a cacophonous litany of curses. She would lambaste Pirouette for such things as leaving too many glasses in her room, though the masquerader was not the dishwashing kind. As punishment, the masquerader withheld juices, laughing derisively. Worst of all for Pirouette, who could withstand such maltreatment, the masquerader would tongue-lash Henri.

"Stargazing dirt-digger!" she scoffed. "Flute fiddler!"

As though his cherished finds were insignificant, which could not be so.

Through light showers, Henri was able to serenade the masquerader until the drizzle subsided. She would snarl sometimes, or groan, but eventually the music calmed her. These times, Pirouette would comb the masquerader's hair, humming and hoping that the real Etoile, wherever she had gone, could sense her faithful presence.

But in torrential downpours such as this, the masquerader was wicked and unsoothable. Though it was beyond Pirouette's comprehension, Henri's love for Etoile never faltered, masquerader or no. Desperate to please her, to find the real Etoile within her, Henri pressed his fingers to the holes of his flute, which was ancient, Chinese. Heavenly music came out from the spaces he did not cover, and Pirouette knew that he had many times called forth the stars this way. But during a heavy rain like this one, the masquerader merely cackled. She plugged her ears and shooed him away. He who she loved so dearly.

That was happening now. Pirouette heard the stop-and-start of the high sweet music. The tremor of each note bespoke Henri's fear and despair, and Pirouette cringed to hear it. A clap of thunder and the shrieking resumed. The masquerader like a banshee in their midst. Pirouette pressed her fingers to her earflaps to block out the keening and the timid, quavering flute. She looked out her upstairs window at the sheet of rain.

Creased and sleepy faces showed in all the other windows. Never had Paris seen such rain, with both thunder and lightning, a brooding sky. The earth began to rumble and shake, as though something momentous might occur. And the water, it rose and rose.

Though it was near morning, Pirouette returned to her bed. She took her fingers from her ears and thought of the willpower she had used to make her second left foot act like a right one. Unswerving. She conjured that image, herself following the long straight line of Leo, and she used it to mute the moans of the masquerader.

She sank into a long delicious rain-drop sleep.

Forty days she slept, and Leo (who feared the masquerader) threw forty pebbles at Pirouette's window, the last so big it should not in fairness be called a pebble. It crashed through the glass and landed beside her on the pillow. She woke and stared at it. As large as her head, it was wet and shining.

"You could have killed me!" she called down to him.

"Or I could have let you be killed!" he hollered back. *"Regarde!"* he demanded, swirling the rising water with his hands.

Pirouette looked. All of Paris was awash with rain, and it was still raining. Indeed, it had begun to seem dangerous. The water had collected in the streets, so it seemed they were all floating in boats, not living in houses. On her own narrow street there were no longer the mossy cobbled stones. They were there, yes, but you could only imagine them beneath the brown swirling water. She thought she saw goldfish swimming by.

And the Seine, it kept rising.

Insane, thought she.

People were flocking now, like flightless birds, flapping to all of the high-up places in Paris. They climbed the flying buttresses of Notre-Dame, and sat hunched with the hunched gargoyles, the fearsome drawing forth those so full of fear. The Tour Eiffel was leaning because there were too many people on one side. The desperate were hanging from the curved iron near the bottom, begging to be pulled up. She thought she saw someone fall and keep falling, but it may have been a swooping bird. She thought of Birdman Reisfeldt, who flew from the parapet way back when. He was a tailor who sewed his cape into wings. He died flying. Died trying, at least.

Would that we could fly today, she mused. Would that we could swim.

"Pirouette!" called Leo.

A fresh swell of water swept in and knocked him sideways. He disappeared and emerged again, further down the street that now was a rushing river.

"Pirouette, you've got to get out of there!" he warned her as the current pushed him away.

This she knew to be true.

Etoile was moaning now beyond compare, her wail a banshee's promise of imminent death in the house. Yes, thought Pirouette. There would be three deaths here if they did not soon vacate.

Pirouette implored the masquerader and Henri.

"The water is rising and rising," she told them.

She pointed to the stairwell to show them how the swirling water had pooled there, but the masquerader refused to look, rolling her eyes back in Etoile's head until only the bloodshot whites showed. A vein in her temple throbbed and throbbed. Henri, he simply sighed. He put his head in his hands the way a turtle hides in his shell.

Pirouette pleaded. She cried in her uncrying way. Still, nothing could make the masquerader step out into the rain, not even the harrowing knowledge that the rain would find her anyway. And nothing could make Henri leave Etoile.

Pirouette trudged back to her room. She flopped on her bed. The pansy wallpaper had begun to curl away from the wall in all four corners. Pirouette herself felt somewhat unglued. In the near distance the white-eyed masquerader had begun to sing in creepy falsetto.

"Rain, rain, go away, come again no other day."

Pirouette plugged her ears.

She worried for the people of Paris. For the paintings in the Louvre, which might soon be lifted from their hooks by rushing water. She worried for *The Kiss*, which, though made from marble, might not withstand such a storm. She worried for the Notre-Dame Cathedral. Home for the *Crown of Thorns*, it had once before been left to rot. She worried for the sprawling gardens which would surely be washed away, the flowers drowning, held by their angel-hair roots under water.

She worried for the animals in the Jardin's little zoo, caged, and some, anyway, unable to swim. And with dismay she wondered where Leo might be. In her mind she saw him tossed up by the waves and then again pulled under. But she had seen his afro repel raindrops. The drops fell on his hair and rested there, like jewels made of water, and then rolled off of him. She hoped against hope that his hair would keep him buoyant, that he could not be in danger of drowning. Still, she donned her swimsuit. Along the scooped neck were peacock fringes that would undulate like fins in the water, each fringe an eye searching for Leo. She sat out on her window ledge, ready to dive. She looked down at her dusty white lap, chapped and itchy, and out at the waterlogged city.

Un, deux, trois . . . and she was squatting now, leaning out, pirouetting through the air and into water.

Ohhh, *l'eau.*

She swam and swam and saw bloodsuckers and octopuses and bright purple starfish and funny plaice with their weird flat bodies. In Paris! She made her way to the Jardin des Plantes and freed the animals from their submarine stables. Some were dead already and only floated when she let them go. Some were fully alive with terror. Slivers of white showed at the edges of their brown animal eyes. The ones who could not swim climbed onto the backs of the ones who could. Where they would swim to she did not know, and realizing this, she felt less heroic to have saved them, to have given them hope.

She swam along boulevard Saint-Germain, up rue Saint-Jacques, along the quai Saint-Michel and across the bridge to Ile de la Cité. She swam deep in the water, passing frantic kicking legs and dog-paddling hands and trying not to conjure her tall narrow home filled with water, water filling Etoile's wailing mouth, water engulfing huge Henri and dislodging the priceless archeological treasures he had blistered his big hands to find. She tried not to conjure water gushing through the holes of the Chinese flute, but she saw it disintegrate before her very mind's eye, becoming all hole. *Horrible, horrible girl,* she thought. She should never have left them behind. And nowhere among the fleeing was Leo. She put her hand to her face, which was so wet from swimming that she almost believed there were tears there.

And yet—something felt different.

She slowed her rapid breaststroke and a wild tress of hair undulated in front of her. She put her hand to her head and held her hair out, staring. Her hair had grown long and shiny, a glimmer of red there. She looked at her hands and feet. The whites of her nails sprouted round from her fingers and toes. So shocked was she, she did not immediately realize that now she was standing, and the water was sinking lower and lower, sucked into the pores of her newly dewy skin. And all the raindrops that fell, fell only on her. Falling slowly, more slowly, and then not at all. Suddenly she felt she was all of herself, whole, twice what she had been.

"Pirouette!" called Leo. "Up here!"

There he stood in all his splendour with an unkempt Babette. Together they clung to the unspinning angel, high upon the Sainte-Chapelle.

All of Paris wished to honour her without delay. Down came the people from their perches, laughing and shouting, *"Merci, chérie!"* They formed a parade and amongst the multitude Pirouette spotted Etoile and Henri, beaming. Right away the city named not just a *rue* for her, but a whole star-shaped traffic circle: Place de Pirouette, which had long been called Place Charles de Gaulle. (Before that it had begun, in some strange twist of fate, as Place de l'Etoile.) In magnificent procession, they marched her towards it along the Champs-Elysées, then around and around and around that circle, and finally through to the Arc de Triomphe.

Oh, she felt triumphant.

Until.

Walking home in her peacock swimsuit, she felt good and bad. Her hair swung with each step and tickled her bare back and shoulders. But she wondered about Charles, whose sign had been so rapidly removed. Surely he had changed the world more dramatically than she ever could. Still, people hooted and hollered. The windows of cafés sprang open and all the city returned to vibrant bustling life. On the surface this was a joyous occasion, but Pirouette knew what she had done and what she had never intended to do. She had swum to save herself and only herself. And also for the quenching delight of swimming. She had not meant to be heroic.

"I feel like a fraud," she whispered to Leo.

"A frog?" said he, momentarily surprised. And then a knowing look came into his mesmerizing eyes. "That's just because you're so full of water."

She thought about correcting him, but now he was on about the strange bulging eyes frogs had, which allowed them to peer above water, and the leathery skin, which looked to be slimy yet was truly quite dry. He blathered on, not even pausing to notice the donkey passing by with a monkey on his back. He talked and talked, all the while following Pirouette's circuitous route, and the ground, it splurched beneath them.

*

Once we went to France, Simon and I. On the walkways that line the Seine there are no railings, only a low stone wall, knee-level, to keep you from tripping into the river. I sat straddling the wall and Simon sat behind me, his arms wrapped around me. Notre-Dame glowed above us with scaffolding up one side and Simon said he wished I could see it without its back brace on. It didn't matter. Everything was so grand and I loved him so much.

Nights were hot and noisy. Simon slept easily through all of it, his leg and his arm thrown over me. He snored, just once, and I put my hand on his shoulder to make him stop. That all it took. It astonished me that he could know my wishes through touch. I lay awake and thought of how lucky I was.

What I most wanted to see was Rodin's house, not for Rodin but for Camille Claudel and also for Lucy, who had tried to shape bodies with her hands. During her sculpture phase, she had told us of Rodin, and of Camille, who'd formed the hands and feet for him. Loved him, and then went crazy. We had known, of course, *La Valse*, the only picture on our wall, and later Lucy had shown us *The Kiss*, never knowing I would one day stand in front of it, thinking of her. The marble bodies looked braided, a man's and a woman's. His hand at her hip with the thumb raised in hesitation. I didn't know if Camille had made that thumb, or the large bony feet, but I thought so. All the passion came from there, from the hands and feet. They were somehow not part of the rest, lifting off and away from the double body. I wondered how it must feel to form a body with your hands, to sense the shoulder taking shape, all the bone and sinew there. How it must have been for them, two people who sculpted bodies, touching each other's. Lucy told us their story before we knew about love or passion. We did not quite understand what she meant, but it made us uncomfortable. She said a love like that was oppressive but rare. When you were in it, you could sometimes not breathe, but once it was gone, you ached all over.

In another room I found *The Waltz*. I had never imagined it might be so small, only eighteen inches high. I stood with my hand over my mouth, I was so overjoyed to see it. My eyes welled up, and when Simon came to where I was standing, I actually said, "Look, isn't it beautiful? My mother had a picture of this when I was a little girl."

But that was all I told him. Together we roamed the museum and the gardens outside. There was a time when art was alive in this place, you could still feel it if you closed your eyes. Rodin and Matisse lived and worked here. Isadora Duncan danced with children in a wing that has since been demolished. The gardens filled up with roses and statues of Adam and Eve.

I bought a postcard of *La Valse*, meaning to send it to Lucy. That night as Simon slept I sat at the table in our room with my pen poised above the blank space. The white curtain blew in and out of the open window, touching the leaded glass. After a long time I put the pen down, tucked the postcard into my guidebook and climbed into bed beside Simon. I had so much to say that I said nothing at all.

CHAPTER IO PARALLEL

Love is all he wants when he calls us. To tell us truly and to hear it echoed back. Some nights he phones us three and four times, swearing he cannot let us go. He says he misses us and wants us home, that he will do anything. Through the holes in the phone his voice sounds strange, like a voice on TV. We listen together, holding the phone between us, not speaking, and when Lucy takes the phone away we can still hear him, a laugh or a cry, we know not which.

He comes to convince us. He has his hair neatly combed, sadly parted. He stands at the door with his coat on, like someone selling something. As if we could close the door and he would disappear. When he comes in Lucy makes tea and he moves around our tiny place and touches the paintings on the walls.

"These are nice," he says.

I think of Wednesdays and the endlessly ringing telephone. When I look at Lucy I see in her eyes that she has missed him. It is surprising to me. I have never thought about whether they are or are not in love, and yet I have known forever the story of their meeting. They were twelve years old, just two years older than me, than you. Until now I have only thought about their lives in relation to mine and yours.

He sits in the beanbag chair and drinks politely from a cup that cost five cents at Goodwill. A little chip and some flowers. We have never seen him drink tea.

Do we hug him?

Yes. I remember his smell. Of soap and shaving lotion. I feel the rasp of his stubble, there despite shaving. I hear the beans shift in the chair as he moves to hold me.

"This is fancy," he says, patting the chair. "Comfy too."

He does not look comfortable. He is too big to just relax and let himself be held by a million beans.

In front is parked the scabby car, rural and out of place on our city street. When we climb in it is too familiar and I close my eyes against it, the four of us each in our right places. He makes us all put belts on, which we never did at home. So timidly he drives, starting and stopping. We jerk with the press of the brakes and he clings to the wheel, looking out, looking up. Cars pass us, honking, and with each blast of a horn I think I could die or just cry for him. We might never make it to the CN Tower.

"Jesus," says Lucy. "Maybe we should've just taken the subway."

Which seems so mean, how could she?

But he only laughs and says, "Yeah, I'm kind of outta my element here."

"Want me to drive?" she asks, and now he laughs so hard he seems like himself again.

We laugh too, and Lucy, because it truly is funny. That time driving, we're all thinking of it:

Lucy at the wheel and us in the back. We were picking him up from work and we were parallel parking, which does not mean what it sounds like it means, not beside but behind, single file. The goal was to fit our car between two cars, and I was struck by the realization that we could not bend or twist. Backwards and forwards we drove in lurching movements, turning now, missing, starting again. Lucy said she must find a back-door handle in her rear-view mirror, that that was how she'd know when to turn. But how much to turn? And for how long? Finally you were sent outside and I could see you through the rear window, holding up your hands to show this much room, that much. Lucy thrust her tongue to the side in concentration. And then I was sent outside too, measuring those distances, and Lucy was in there alone, yanking the wheel, laughing a laugh we couldn't hear. That was how he found us. Lucy didn't see him until he rapped on the glass, "Need some help, lady?" and he opened the door and her hysterical laughter came tumbling out. He scooped her out too, flopped her over his shoulder, her orange hair wild and swinging. Upside down, she was more delirious than ever.

Where did *that* him go? Is he back with us now?

We park and we walk to the tower, which grows and grows.

He points up at it. "Betcha she's got about a twelve-foot sway on a windy day."

How silly he looks here on Front Street, wearing his boots in so little snow, the tongues flapping out. Here the men wear fine dark suits that are unlike his one suit, which he does not wear now, thank God—he would look even sillier in comparison. His suit, worn for special occasions, is the same one he wears in the photo that shows Lucy as his bride. Her grin so wide in that picture she looks almost insane. "Crazy in love," that's what she told us. She is wearing white, like a normal bride. A strand of pearls so close on her neck that I wonder, will they pop when she swallows? All those shining pearls flying loose and rolling.

Now we are holding hands in the windowed elevator, and in our hearts is such excitement I can feel the double beat in our palms. They are behind us, Lucy and Dad, and we are pushed closer to the glass by many strangers crowding on. Up we rise too quickly, stomachs turning. Further above than ever we'd been below. So small is this city! I think only now of the wind, the twelve-foot sway, but it seems impossible that anything bad might happen in the presence of so many people. And our father is here, watching over us.

When we get to the top there is nowhere to go but around. He slides coins into the slot of the telescope until we have found our house, our school, all the places we know. It gives a new order, to look from above at the smallness of things. I think of when I lost you in Chinatown: *This is where we'll come if we ever get separated. Here is where we'll find each other again.*

And here we all are.

Afterwards we take him to Chinatown. He is our tourist. He has never before eaten anything Chinese except egg rolls and sweet 'n' sour chicken balls, and so we show him sticky buns and dumplings and wormy noodles in a black-bean sauce, which we know all about because we have been here many times with Lucy and also because at school we have a Chinese friend, Helena Ying, who brings real Chinese food in her lunch box.

"I think we've got us a couple of city girls here, Luce," he says, smiling.

Oh, his happy smile.

I want to say, Please can we come home now? Because here people live on the streets, you see. Every day is garbage day—the bags piled up make a wall. Yesterday a man shot his wife in the stomach and killed the baby growing there. We heard it on the radio, between songs. Every day something happens, Daddy. The floating germs are invisible, they might be all over us, inside us by now. I am careful not to touch, but Eugenie touches everything, you know. See her now, she is running her hands along the underside of the table, and who knows what has been there, who knows who?

That whole day he stays. That whole night. Husband and wife, he sleeps in her room. We can hear them laughing until it is no longer night but morning. In and out of sleep we drift, dreaming of home. I think once of the ghost, but with him here we are so safe we can't ever be frightened.

In the morning is a fight. We do not use glasses to hear it. We lie in our beds, each looking at the matching blank face of the other. The voices gentle now, but we know they will change.

"We can't come back because of one good day."

"There will be more good days. I promise."

A pause.

"Luce," he says, so grave. "Luce. Gimme a chance. Give *us* a chance."

"I just can't see how anything would really change."

Now he says nothing.

"I want a different kind of life," she says. And more quietly, "I want to be an artist."

Then comes an awful laugh.

"Is this what you call being an artist? Painting apples and working at a drugstore? If so, you can be an artist at home. We've got two drugstores there and app—"

"No," she says flatly. "No, I can't."

Nothing.

And then his voice: "Fuck you."

Without even seeing him, I can envision the vein in his forehead. The very pulse of it is violent. You blink slowly and turn to look at the window. I put my pillow over my head. Inside are feathers from a duck or a goose. We have never eaten a duck or a goose, but people do, Helena Ying might. In Chinatown they hang dead in the store windows, stretched, strangely orange. Wishbones inside.

What if we had gone then? What if we had just said, yes, we'll go. We'll try. We will all try. She had said, *I just can't see how anything would really change,* but now, as she came to the end of her life, could she? Could she see how everything might have changed? If this had not happened or that. If we had not eaten the candy apples and he had not found their wrappers. If we had always been quiet and good. If she had. If he had not turned homeward that day at Golden Lake and all four of us had just gone and kept on going and never gone back again. Singing to the radio. If, if, if. We rarely know it at the time, but every decision we make has the potential to alter the direction of our lives, or ever so swiftly end them.

He is wearing his coat and he is standing at the door, like he did yesterday, and I think for a minute somebody might laugh and say, "Okay, let's try this again." But no one laughs. He leaves without us, offering so little in the way of words or touch that I wonder if I might still be dreaming. Through frost on the high-up window I watch him go. If he can see my forehead and eyes, my hand waving, he does not show me.

Nevertheless I want to be with him all that long drive, though I know you do not, Eugenie. You love the weightless happiness of our life without him, the absolute absence of anger and the surprises that come from no rules. For me, it is as though we live without walls or roads, we never know where we are going or if we are properly dressed for such a journey. When Lucy says we are going to Kensington Market, we could very well end up miles away, in a cemetery called Mount Pleasant, which is pleasant, yes, but not in the cold and the rain. Because we are exact opposites, it is only me, on the day he leaves, who wants to be with him on the 401, the widest road in the world, and then on the smaller roads, two lanes only, worn-out grey. Halfway we'd go through a drive-through for burgers and fries and eat the hot salty food while we drove, heading home.

All that visit you were waiting for the snap, the moment he would screw up. You couldn't see how much he loved us. I couldn't see how much you knew.

That night we gather in the bathroom, as though it is any other night. I feel sick that no one cares he has gone. Come and gone, and now it is as if he has never been here at all. *Here*. He was here in the home we have without him and we let him go away. Told him, *Go away*.

We are brushing our teeth and Lucy is taking a bath, as though everything is normal.

"A rat could come up through the toilet," you say with your toothpaste mouth.

You heard it at school, from Helena. A girl she knew had been bathing and had seen a rat rise up in the bowl. Not just wet but greasy.

"If she had been peeing," you tell us, "it might have bitten her. She could have died," you say, grinning.

I stare into the green bowl of our toilet, which has a ring that cannot be scrubbed clean.

"Oh, baloney," says Lucy.

But it does not seem like baloney to me.

It makes me afraid for a long time to pee. I long for our other home, our father. There were no rats there, it was a different world. There were mice sometimes, but these were mostly dead when we saw them, downy grey bodies lying sleepily on their sides. Killed by cats who had only been playing. Here a rat is a danger. By day it might live in the sewers, in the subway tunnels, but at night it foraged, thinking garbage was food.

I begin to watch for them. When I pee I do not sit down, not at school, not at home. I hover above the seat and look unblinking into the bowl. I will always be ready. How can you go on as usual, Eugenie? I see rats everywhere. Disguised as squirrels roaming free in the park, people feeding them. I see through the plumes of their tails another tail, stiff and thin. Their fat greedy bodies disgust me. Rats will eat anything.

Once, in a park, you said, "Imagine living only on chestnuts."

That was earlier, the time of year when chestnuts fall from the trees in their prickled green outfits. For us, it was miraculous—there was no such tree where we came from. What had they eaten, I wonder, the small red squirrels who lived in the walls at Uncle William's? Pine cones? Keys from the maple trees? Here the squirrels used their minuscule hands to pry the green layer open and inside was a jewel, the polished brown shell of the chestnut like glossed wood, with a circling grain. This too they pried open, to eat the meat inside, and aloud you wondered, "Why don't the weird-eyes eat them?"

"Maybe they taste bad," I said.

"They can't," you said. You held your palms up so they faced the sky, and you shrugged your shoulders. It was a gesture that was Lucy's. "What about chestnuts roasting on an open fire? They never would've written a song about a nut that wasn't delicious."

"It's not a song about a nut," I said.

"What's it about then?"

That I didn't know. Just now I could not remember anything more than that line and another: *folks dressed up like Eskimos.* But I knew it was not about that either.

"Let's test them," you said. "If they're good, we'll collect them and give them out."

They were everywhere, after all. Free and falling from trees throughout the city, enough for squirrels and man alike. From the ground you chose two and peeled away the prickled outer layers, then passed mine to me. The shells were hard to open, hard as wood. With our teeth we bit them loose until the cream nut showed, and then we bit that, tasting chalk and mould.

You shook your head and tossed the nut away. "Maybe they've tasted them already."

Later we learned these chestnuts were not the same as the ones you could buy, which came all the way from Italia, home of Maria Rosa Carmelita. Because of the horrible taste, we wondered if perhaps you could get very sick, even die from eating these, and it seemed mysterious to me that a squirrel's body could tolerate what ours could not.

The squirrels nowadays were mottled and strange. As I wandered through Toronto I wished you could see them. Red, black and grey all at once. I thought about how sprawling and dangerous this city had seemed in our childhood. Since those days, everyone had made their way here. The downtrodden were scarce then, compared to the multitudes now.

CHAPTER II DOUBLY LOVELY

In the days after our father's visit we fight over the mess that spills out from under your bed. All your things—your balled-up socks and your inside-out clothes—are inching towards me. I kick them back to you and tell you to clean up your mess. This is a nothing kind of fight, but there is something else inside it, something bigger. Like the things under your bed, it seeps out, and though we never mention it, it is this something else that makes our faces red-hot angry. You are a no-good fighter with words, though I could go on that way forever. I call you "slob," "sloth," "lazy," and throw a sock at you. It flies in your face and bounces off, and that is the moment you can't stand me any more. You fly forward. Your palms slam against my chest and I land on the floor, looking up at you. Your blotched face, your shoulders heaving, your little pinched mouth. Wisps of hair floating out from your pigtails.

In these same days, the bickering aftermath, Lucy takes down all of her paintings and bundles them and puts them out with the trash. *La Valse* stays pinned to the wall, but other than this, she says the bare walls are more beautiful, and after all, she painted those too. She does not say it but we know she is disheartened. We can see that in her eyes, a duller blue. Even her hair seems less bright and now remains unbraided, uncurled with that dreadful used curling iron. Wednesdays, now, she stays home. She says she had hoped to make moving lives, not still ones.

But she is forever bringing home books from the library, stacks of them depicting art from the beginning of time. Sometimes she reads out loud and shows us pictures, for instance of Icarus drowning. We would not have seen if she had not pointed to his naked legs sinking into the water. His melted wings are nowhere, and the whole world goes on without him. Boats drift by and a farmer ploughs. A shepherd and his sheep meander. This book holds Icarus and the maudlin madonnas, and also Vincent van Gogh and his swirling blue amoebas of night. We begin to forget our own squabbles and ask for the tortuous story of his ear but she shrugs us off.

"Art is not about Vincent's ear," she says. "Look what a thick book this is. It goes back to the beginning of time, before the Biddenden maids and beyond. Ever since people grew hands they have made things."

We laugh but we see she is crying. Just like that she is in pieces. The book lies open on her lap and great tears drop on the paper, wrinkling the page, which is thin, made from onions. We don't know how to help, what to do, and so we stand watching. We have no idea what is wrong.

Whenever I thought about Lucy and her art—whether it was papier-mâché bodies or the pig's head—I thought about the stories she told, real but retaining the essence of fairy tales. As an adult I had come to believe that this was what she searched for, what she hoped to show us in a million different ways: a magic that was truthful and a truth that was magical.

She always said that as twins we were so inseparable we may as well have been joined at the hip, thus the stories she told were wild tales of togetherness; they had the most desolate endings. Nevertheless, they were true.

"Cross my heart," she says, as nightly she brushes our hair. Our hair is not like her bright hair. It is thin, dull blonde, but she says the brushing can change that, bring on shine and lustre, and we believe her. Before we leave for the city, before we ever even think we'll leave for the city, leaving him behind, she brushes our hair and then lies with us in our room and tells us these stories, both happy and sad, and we lie listening.

Where is he?

There is no sound of TV or radio, no sound of his voice, which echoes too loud through the house. Only Lucy's voice, and behind that the sound of our breathing—sometimes no sound because we are holding our breath as the stories unfold.

I am in bed, and you are in your bed above me. Flannel sheets sticking to my flannel nightgown, so now it is winter, we are nine years old. This nightgown, it has lace trim on the collar and cuffs, but yours, matching, has none; you've cut away the trim. "Too itchy," you said when I saw you with the scissors in your hands. Now at your sleeves and neckline the flannel is frayed and unravelling.

"Do cows ever have twins?" we ask.

Lucy knows everything. She is Our Lady of Information.

"Do dogs? Do cats?"

"Once," says Lucy, "there was a cat with two heads and seven legs."

"So two cats?"

"Yes," she says. "Two cats in one. You should have heard it meow!"

"*Them*, you mean!"

Lucy grins. In our room there is a loveseat, garish and purple, and she sprawls there swaying her gangly legs, which are hooked over the armrest. Above her the blue-and-green lamp casts blue-and-green light on her too-big pyjamas, a man's, our father's. She twists her long braid around her wrist like a bracelet.

"There have even been two-headed turtles and fish and snakes," she says. "Joined at birth and together forever."

"Freaks?"

She shrugs. "I suppose. Freaks of nature."

I try to picture that frightened two-headed turtle, unable to pull his heads into his lone shell's small hole.

"The Biddenden maids were freaks of nature too, if that's what you choose to call them. They were heiresses to a modest fortune, lucky girls."

"Lucky?"

"Yeah! If they'd been poor, maybe no one would ever have known about them. They were joined at the hip and walked everywhere with an arm around the other. When one died, the other pleaded not to be separated from her. For hours she lay with her dead sister at her side, until finally she also died. And when she went she whispered, 'As we came together, so we will also go together.'"

Our faces blanched and our mouths hung open.

"The maids were very generous," Lucy continued, "but they were also a bit vain."

"You mean they thought they were pretty?"

"Sure!" says Lucy. "And rightly so—they were very pretty."

"But they were freaks!"

"Yes, and it made them doubly lovely. They couldn't bear the thought of vanishing from the earth without anyone ever laying eyes on them again. So when they died they left their land to the church with the stipulation that, each Easter, cakes bearing their image be distributed among the people."

I do not like those Biddenden maids. Making cakes of themselves! Who would want to eat those cakes, with two faces on each, two conceited joined bodies? Instead, lonely Edward is my constant favourite. Time after time, I ask Lucy to tell this story of a boy with an angelic face at the front, but the cruel and hideous face of a stranger at the back.

"Poor Edward," says Lucy. "He was so terribly ashamed of his deformity that he locked himself away in his room and rarely saw anyone, not even his own family. Alone up there—well, not really alone, but you know what I mean—the face talked on and on to him in a hissing whisper. And he could never really see it or know it—confront it face to face! No, he could never be rid of it. He was the only one who could hear its wheezy voice, but others had seen the pasty lips move, so no one believed he was crazy. Only unfortunate. But how crazy that voice eventually made him! Poor Edward, he was a truly gifted musician, and he strummed his lute and sang his songs loudly to drown out the voice of that strange babbling twin."

"A twin? It was a twin?"

"Well, sure—in a way it was. Separate from him but part of him too. Anyway, it talked on and on, and Edward would never say what evil things it told him, so people assumed the words were so horrible they could not be repeated."

"What did it say to him?"

"I don't know what it said to him."

"But what do you *think*?"

"I don't *know* what to think. That's just the point— nobody knew! A thing like that just can't be supposed."

"Make something up!"

"Please!" Lucy says with disgust. "A body can't just *make something up* right in the middle of a true story!" Lucy pauses, looking long at me and then at you. "Please," she says again. "And that's what Edward said too," she tells us, reclaiming her story voice: "*'Please!'* he begged the doctors. 'Remove it!' But that face was so entwined with the workings of his own fine brain that amputation was impossible, and in the end Edward, lonely Edward, swallowed poison and died, and only then did the whispering cease."

It is my secret that some nights I dream I love Edward, and in my dream I see myself, hearts circling my

head as I look upon him. He is tall and glorious, a tor-
tured soul. I touch his face, his hair, and when my hand
reaches the back of his head I feel that other crazy face
there, the face of the evil twin, its lips parted in maniacal
laughter.

You, your favourite story is always changing, you can
never make up your mind about anything.

"The Biddenden maids are my favourite!" you say
this night, and I, below you, roll my eyes, because I know
that tomorrow night you will say, "I love the Two-
Headed Nightingale the absolute best of all!"

Is this that story she's about to recite, about Millie-
Christine, eighth wonder of the world, when finally we
hear him? The lit-up face of the clock shows five past
two, so, oh, he's been drinking. *It's too late*, he will yell in
a voice that shocks with its loudness. *It's way too fuckin'
late for those girls to be up. What kind of mother are you?*
He'll open the door to our blue-and-green room, letting
in cold white light from the hallway and also that smell
that comes with him, not just from his breath but pores
too, a smell still there in the morning.

Sometimes, though I loved you, I wished I was an only
child. I have never told anyone that but you knew. There
were times we read each other's every thought, and on
the days we felt too opposite I sent those thoughts right
to you. Ever after I would tell myself it was a normal

thing, the fleeting wish of a child, that you wished it too, I knew you had, but the ball of guilt grew inside me when you were truly gone. Simon once told me that as a child he had wished for brothers, three of them, because everyone wants what they've never had, especially if they know they can't get it.

"Did you ever wish for sisters?" he asked, and for a moment I was so confused I was speechless.

"Sure," I said finally. And I made up a story to support that lie.

In fact, of course, what I wished for was the opposite. I wished I was the only child of a man and a woman who were normal. I would have long hair and a long name. Jane was a plain and ugly name and did not match Eugenie. If I could, I would have chosen something glorious like Maria Rosa Carmelita. I would not have chosen a name that began with *J*, which was not even formally accepted into the alphabet until the nineteenth century. For hundreds of years it was simply the consonant form of *I*, a ghostly twin struggling for its own place. Descended from the Greek iota, so tiny it almost meant nothing. Perhaps I would have called myself Dulcimer-Gossamer, my secret favourite name. A girl with a name like that would have to be a miracle child. Not a genius or a saint or a princess, but miraculous just the same.

DULCIMER-GOSSAMER

Cliché and Bob were so old they were white-haired and balding. Before their baby arrived they had given up all hope of conceiving, thus at her miraculous birth they believed she was regal and divine—deserving, even—and bestowed upon her a fitting name. She was born with a dulcimer laugh and one fine strand of gossamer hair—white, like theirs—and so they called her Dulcimer-Gossamer.

But it did not grow, that strand. Not for a long, long time. And no other strands grew round it. Cliché and Bob joked that she took after them, and it was funny, at first, that they were a tufty threesome. And then, less funny. Portraits of them graced the family mantel and showed the transformation of Dulcimer-Gossamer from burbling baby to teetering tot to miserable, inconsolable girl—for she by now knew others: Sophia, whose blonde swinging hair caught the light from the sun. She had seen the dark tumbling curls of Lillian, and marvelled at the blue in that blackness. She had seen Marilyn and Ruth, twin strawberry blondes, and she had wished for hair that took its name from a fruit. For she had also seen her own self in the mirror and deduced that to have sparse hair was to have sparse happiness. Perhaps no happiness. Certainly no braids, no buns, no pigtails. All over she ached, longing for ringlets.

"Come, come now," said Cliché. "You can't compare apples and oranges."

Which made no sense, because yes, you could. You could say that oranges were orange and apples were not, but that both were fruit. You could say that one had a tasty peel, and the other's was bitter and strange, but that both were brightly coloured. You could say that orange started with *o* and apple started with *a*, but that both began with vowels. There was no end to the comparisons you could make.

Often her mother struggled to comfort her. "Beauty is in the eye of the beholder," she told Dulcimer-Gossamer. "Good things come in bald packages."

But Cliché's words were tired and empty, and Dulcimer-Gossamer rolled her eyes, unsoothed.

"You are magnificent anyway," said her father, trying. "You are delightful regardless."

But Dulcimer-Gossamer did not want to be magnificent anyway or delightful regardless. She wanted to be simply magnificent and delightful.

Each night she slept with that lone silky strand wrapped tightly round her finger, tugging just lightly, wishing it long. But nothing worked. Each morning she awoke and rushed to the mirror and she did not laugh that dulcimer laugh when she looked upon her near-bald reflection there. Rather, she spoke to it.

"I would give my eye-teeth—" she began.

Her reflection guffawed musically. "Oh, come off it," it told her. "You would not."

Dulcimer-Gossamer paused. "My right arm?"

"Pants-on-fire!" said her reflection. The voice was sing-song and mean. But it spoke the truth, and Dulcimer-Gossamer could not deny it. She did not want the beauty that came with luxurious tresses only to have it marred by a gap-toothed smile or a missing limb.

"Okay, okay," she said. She pressed her finger to her cheek and thought hard. "My laugh," she said finally. "I would give my dulcimer laugh for a full head of fabulous hair."

One eyebrow shot up in that reflection of hers. "You should watch what you wish for, missy."

Yet, wisp by wisp it grew. She felt the traces of tresses with her fingers first, and then ran to the mirror to behold the new hair, fine and bright white, like the web of a spider.

Ohhh!" she moaned. "I'm beautiful!"

"Yes, except—" her reflection began, but Dulcimer-Gossamer had stopped listening.

Longer and longer grew the strands, and Dulcimer, too, grew comely. She fashioned her spider-web hair into the most outrageous styles, spinning star-shaped webs that sprang from her head in every direction.

"Each one is different!" cried Cliché, admiring. "Like a snowflake!"

Dulcimer-Gossamer glowed with joy. She found she could add trailing ribbons and rubies and blooms of flowers without having to bother fastening them: anything she put onto the web stuck and remained stuck until she, Dulcimer-Gossamer herself, pulled it off. Which she would do oh so gently because her hair was astonishingly fine and delicate.

Because she was beautiful, she was happy, and because she was happy, she laughed always, not minding that the sound was no longer that dulcimer sound for which she had been named. It shocked her at first. A giggle spurted out as she was admiring her reflection and the sound of it was so grating that her hands flew to her ears.

"What was that?" she asked her reflection.

"*That,*" replied her reflection, "was *you.*"

It gave her pause. But only briefly.

"Oh," she said. And laughed again. And winced. And laughed again. And decided, twirling a tress around her finger, that it was not so bad a laugh at all.

(In fact it was harsh and whiny. If it had to be compared to an instrument, it would be compared to the bagpipes. And that was what people called her behind her back.

Behind her over-large do. They called her Bagpipe-Gossamer, B. G. for short.)

Blonde Sophia stopped calling without explanation. Lillian had always been afraid of the bagpipes, and so she ran and hid whenever Dulcimer-Gossamer approached. Marilyn and Ruth were identical snobbish debutantes, and Dulcimer-Gossamer could only suppose they were jealous of her now, and thus distanced themselves. She told her reflection she didn't care.

"I don't give a hoot," she said. "Not a whit or a darn or even a rat's—"

"But won't you be blue?" asked her reflection.

Dulcimer-Gossamer laughed and winced. "Nope," said she. "You don't need friends to be happy." She poofed her do with the palm of her hand. "You only need hair."

Cliché and Bob, aging, balding and just a smidgeon wiser than their daughter, were filled with woe to see such arrogance emerge in their little darling. That her dulcimer laugh seemed gone forever dismayed them. Still, they wanted her to be happy, and so did everything they could to accommodate her—and her enormous coiffure, which grew and grew, posing problems. The girl could not get through doorways, for instance, without snagging her webs, which greatly upset her. Cliché and Bob believed the only answer was to widen the doors of their house so Dulcimer-Gossamer could roam freely without any harm coming to her elaborate pompadour. And because they were wealthy, they paid for the widening of all the doors in the town's shops, so that Dulcimer-Gossamer could wander where she pleased, buying up baubles and blooms for her do. But she did not know they were behind all the renovations, and she believed the whole town had made an immense collaborative effort to befriend her (well, everyone except Sophia, Lillian, Marilyn and Ruth). This she appreciated, but not too much: she told her reflection she would have done the same thing had the web been on another head. Certain people were meant to be admired. Certain people were wooed by the population at large. And she, of late, was a Certain Person.

Her favourite stop was the flower shop. Each week, she shopped for fresh blooms with which to decorate her do. A fragrant pink peony in her centre-web brought such delight she could not stop laughing that laugh! And the laugh itself just made her laugh harder. (Which no one seemed to mind. Hadn't they all widened their doors for her?) But how it annoyed her to wander through the shop and feel her webs catch on the dead flowers, which hung from the ceiling just like vulgar dead chickens at the butcher's.

"You know," she told the florist, adding a laugh to mellow her words, "I really do not relish dead flowers in my hair."

"Relish?" he asked. "You want relish in your hair?"

"No!" hissed Dulcimer-Gossamer. "I said I cannot abide dead flowers in my hair!"

"No?" said he.

"No," said she. Adding "Ha-ha" as sincerely as she could, for Dulcimer-Gossamer knew how to get her way. ("You'll catch more bees with honey," that was what her mother always said. And yet, why would she want to catch bees? Sometimes her mother said the craziest things.)

Dulcimer-Gossamer tapped her foot. She waited for his response.

But the florist simply wrapped her peony and held his hand out for money.

Dulcimer-Gossamer hesitated. "They stick," she said. She pointed at the brittle bits high upon her hair. "To my webs."

"Oh?" said he.

"Yes!" said she. "Tee-hee," she added, remembering the bees.

Still he held his palm out.

Ooooh! She did not feel like laughing. She dropped the money in his hand and stormed towards the door, pausing there a moment. "I suppose you think since you've done *this*," she said, pointing to the widened door frame, "that you've done enough for me already!"

"Yes," said the florist. He paused and held a gardenia to his nose, sniffing. "As a matter of fact, I do."

Oo-hooh! So mad was she her webs were shaking. And when she got home it took forever to remove all those bits of dead flowers from her hair. How she hated dead flowers! They were insipid! Musty! Déclassé!

Exhausted from her anger, and from all the time spent with her delicate arms raised to her delicate sullied hair, Dulcimer-Gossamer fell fast asleep. She did not even change into her nightgown. She did not even put her treasured pink peony in water. She did not even emit that one last bagpipe giggle of happiness that always escaped from her princess-like lips just as she drifted off into sleep.

And that was when the worst thing happened.

That peony was filled with ants, and late in the night they emerged from between the fragrant pink petals. They crawled in a thin black line along Dulcimer-Gossamer's bedside table, and then down the side of the table, and then onto the floor, and then up the leg of her bed, and then onto her shoulder, and then onto her pretty face, and then into her fancy webs. And then—nowhere. They were stuck! The tragic truth was that if she had laughed her bagpipe laugh, it might have scared the ants away before they ever got near her webs, but Dulcimer-Gossamer had been in no mood for laughing. Nor was she come morning, when she rose to gaze upon her radiant reflection and saw that her fine white hair was black with ants.

Dulcimer-Gossamer sobbed and wailed and her reflection cackled meanly.

"Stop laughing!" she cried.

"I can't!" roared her reflection, laughing harder.

A laughing ant
Cannot recant
A laugh whose laugh
Remains extant.

"Stop it!" cried Dulcimer-Gossamer.

Dear B.G., I can't, I say.
You look like one big ant today!

"Stop! Stop rhyming!"
But her reflection, as Cliché would say, was on a roll.

Webs are always sticky.
They're meant for trapping prey.
You must chop off all your hair
To shoo those ants away.

"I said *stop!*"

No you won't be fancy.
You'll be without your do.
But underneath your scalp of pink
You'll still at heart be you.

Moaning, Dulcimer-Gossamer ran from her cruel rhyming reflection.

But it was no use.

Everyone said the same thing: *You must chop off all your hair to shoo those ants away.*

Her father said it. Her mother said it.

"Nooo!" wailed Dulcimer-Gossamer. "I wooon't!"

"Come, come now," said Cliché. "Perhaps it will grow back! And if not, it's not the end of the world!"

Which was untrue, for what was a world without hair? Without baubles and braids and bows and bangs and barrettes and beehive bouffants? Without ringlets? And why would it grow back, when she had had to wheel and deal to get it in the first place? What had she to trade now?

"Nooo!" she cried again, to no one and everyone at once.

And ran sobbing to her room, where there was that glinting glass bowl filled with butterfly clips and streams of satin ribbon hanging from her mirror and the fancy comb-and-brush set with its long porcelain handles, and the scrunchies which were for casual ponytails, and the pink sponge rollers that formed such gentle curls, and a long row of bobby pins, each with a jewel at the bend. And a peony. Lying limp, now, on her bedside table. Everywhere, everything reminding her. The mirror, too, which showed her reflection. She was pig-eyed from crying.

"Boo-hoo," said her reflection, which Dulcimer-Gossamer chose to ignore.

There was a tap on the door.

"Dulcie?"

It was Cliché.

Tap-tap-tap. And another noise. The snip of scissors? Yes, she was sure she heard it!

"Dulcie!"

Snip-snip.

She could not and would not give in. And so she did the craziest thing: out her window she went, like a princess eloping alone. She used the lattice for a ladder, and she climbed down the side of the house, crushing clematis blooms as she went and saying, "Sorry, sorry, sorry," to each one, for once she had loved to pluck them and place them in her webs. Barefoot, she ran across the grass and hopped the fence and fled down the hill and into the woods, and wandered under a rustling canopy of leaves that let in only pieces of the sky. Not knowing where she was going or why, she walked until she could not walk any longer, for her naked feet were swollen and sore, having been poked by pine needles and bitten by bugs.

Ugh, she thought. Bugs. She wondered how many ants were here, in the woods, and she thought, with a little giggle and a brief lifting of spirit, that however many there had been, now, with her presence, there were more.

She leaned against a tree, and the bark, which should have felt rough, felt comfy as a pealess feather bed because of her fatigue. She was so worn out that she did not mind when it began to rain lightly. In fact, she liked the drip-drop-drip of the rain on the leaves, which formed a huge umbrella above her. Soon she slept and dreamed of that sound, in harmony with the layered songs of cicadas, tree frogs and katydids. Dreamed too of the lifted wings of spotty ladybugs, June bugs, butterflies and moths. Of dragonflies with their four long iridescent wings and their eyes which hide thousands of smaller eyes. She dreamed of these and of damselflies, bumblebees, centipedes, millipedes, caterpillars and, yes, of spiders too. She dreamed that she was lying there, dreaming, and that a spider came along and saw her dozing. Enamoured of her wild ant-filled webs, the spider set to work spinning a mansion, weaving its own gossamer strands into those of Dulcimer-Gossamer's so that, when the spinning was done, Dulcimer-Gossamer was firmly fastened to the tree, unable to turn this way or that, unable to stand or stretch or meander or shop or—

Oh!

She awoke with a start. And found that, no, it had not been a dream but the truth, for here she was—stuck. As she had never been stuck before.

She looked ridiculous. *More* ridiculous than she had earlier, which she would never have thought possible. She knew because she could see her many reflections in the little beads of rainwater that graced the web. A web that had once been hers but now was the palatial home of a spider. The web stretched over every branch, and even formed a passageway to the tree beside.

Dulcimer-Gossamer's pretty mouth hung open in shock, and her many reflections grinned meanly.

"Ohhh nooo!" she cried.

"Ahhh yesss!" the reflections chorused.

At these foreign sounds in the woods, the spider, on a nearby branch, turned and paused in its frenzied weaving.

"Hello!" it said. "And welcome. You've given me a wonderful idea!"

Dulcimer-Gossamer moaned in dismay, and her many reflections cackled, rhyming a nasty rhyme.

Tit for tat! What a hat!

At this, Dulcimer-Gossamer was filled with violent anger and superhuman strength. She glared at her reflections, and then at the spider, and she pulled and pulled until her hair-holes stung.

"*Stop!*" cried the spider, hurrying, scurrying, almost flying towards her on his tight-rope webs. "*Please stop!*"

The look on his spider face, the horror in his black spider eyes, froze her. She sat staring at those widened eyes, and suddenly she saw her reflection in them. It was not laughing, nor rhyming in its evil way. It simply looked, unblinking, back at her. And then it spoke.

"Ponder the lowly spider, who must begin all over again, spinning and respinning his elaborate web each time someone unwittingly walks through it or tears it away on purpose."

"But—" began Dulcimer-Gossamer, speaking quietly. "But what about me? What shall I do? I cannot live here in the woods. I cannot survive, glued to this tree. Nothing to eat, nothing to do, nowhere to pee."

She looked into those spider eyes and waited.

"Surely," said her calm reflection, "if a spider can spin a web, it can unspin you from one."

"Yes!" said the spider eagerly. "I can and I will if you'll let me!"

Panic welled in Dulcimer-Gossamer. "But then I would be bald!" she cried. "I will *not* give up my webs!" And at this she pulled and pulled again, anxious to free herself from the tree, from the imploring eyes of the spider and, mostly, from her own deploring eyes within them.

"Please!" cried the spider. "Never have I known a home so grand," the spider told her. "When I saw your webs, sullied though they are, I was filled with architectural inspiration. I could not stop weaving! If you were to tear yourself from this tree now, both my masterpiece and your do would be utterly destroyed."

At this, the spider shed a tear, and in that tiny tear Dulcimer-Gossamer saw yet another reflection. Oh, would she never be rid of herself? She looked away, up at the leaves, but the webs and the reflecting raindrops were there too. Straight ahead and all around. She closed her eyes and sighed. And when she opened them again, everyone was still there, waiting. The spider and all the little Dulcimer-Gossamers resting in the web, bouncing lightly in the breeze, which was cool and gentle, smelling of rain. She noticed for the first time how intricate the web itself was. Finer than hers had ever been, bereft though it was of jewels and ribbons.

"Okay," she said, despondent. "Unspin me."

And while the spider detached the web from Dulcimer-Gossamer's head, her reflections looked on proudly. In them she could see her eyes welling up, for she was sorrowful beyond belief. But she did not sob out loud, and she did not speak. She simply waited. She could feel a lightness, a lifting of burdens, for such a large web, though made from gossamer, was not a weightless load. It was nice, that lightness. A relief, almost. But she felt something else too. A tickling. The little feet of the spider and his unspinning spinnerets were tickling her, and she began to giggle uncontrollably, laughing a dulcimer laugh. If she had looked at her many reflections just then, she would have discovered a miracle: she would have been able to see that laugh, for it danced and curled around her head, unrolling and rolling up like butterfly tongues, like springing rainbow ringlets. But Dulcimer-Gossamer, for once, was not looking at herself. All she was doing was laughing. It was laughter that from now on would cause every doorway to widen magically in welcome.

For now she was magnificent. And she was delightful.

*

Everyone thought it was a story for children but it was not necessarily that.

"Why is it that grown-ups reject storybooks with pictures?" I asked.

Simon shrugged. "They don't all," he said.

For this story, he had created mazes from Dulcimer-Gossamer's hair. The little book came with a pencil attached; you were meant to draw your way out of the labyrinth.

CHAPTER 12 **ALICE AND ALICE**

I walked through Little Italy and tried to recall the Italian words Simon taught me, one sentence, rolling *r*'s, lilting vowels. It had made me think of Miss Reese at the time, though of course I didn't tell him.

We lived in this neighbourhood for such a short while, you and me and Lucy, yet it had been stretched into eternity in my memory. Some things seemed the same. On the side streets were the brick houses and tiny yards, statues of Mary there. The bare grey twigs of rose bushes which would bloom again in garish pink and red. I remembered that some blossoms held out almost until Christmas, and it was so surprising to see them. Our town was too far north for flowers in winter. I remembered too the old Italian ladies all in black, mourning forever. They were still here, like me from another time and place.

Other things were different. College Street now was lined with bars and restaurants. Near the corner of Crawford Street, where we had lived, was a sprawling video store. I couldn't remember what had been there before, but I knew it had been something smaller, less fluorescent.

As I walked down our old street I could feel myself become smaller too, your small self beside me, Alice and Alice in Wonderland. The house was still crooked. The patchy grass had been dug up, replaced with red shale, and I could not see into the window because now there was a Canadian flag hanging there. But in my mind we are kneeling in the dirt and cupping our hands to the glass, looking in on Lucy. The home she has made appears make-believe, with its orange-peel walls, the voluminous beanbag chair and the table that is not a table but an old door on horses. She always says you can make a place special with things you find, more special than if you were to buy proper matching things, and so we bring home what others have discarded—mismatched kitchen chairs, battered picture frames, which we hang empty now that Lucy's paintings have been taken down—and also rocks, chestnuts, snails' shells, acorns.

Sometimes we are happy.

Christmas comes and we buy a tree, a thing we never knew one could do. We do not go home because Lucy says it is time to make new traditions. At first I am appalled, but then we string coloured lights back and forth across the ceiling and leave them on while we are sleeping. We make a tangled ball of lights and hang it like glowing mistletoe by the door. That is amazing to me, that tangle. If I can keep his picture from my mind, I do not miss him much, but when it creeps in I am sad and sorry, sure that we will not be forgiven.

And he phones and phones. I know he asks to come because I hear her crying.

"It doesn't work," she says. "You just get angry."

For the first time ever we have spaghetti for Christmas dinner. I am sucking the long noodles into my mouth and I am almost crying because I can see him at Grandma and Grandpa's, where there is a fake white tree, where he is a boy again, and lonely.

And at night you fall asleep beneath the coloured lights and I, beside you, look at the little window, white with frost. I think of the ghost and our missing father, and wonder what is a ghost if not the absence of someone? I feel the ghost all around me now, and want to wake you and tell you I know what you mean. I turn on my side and watch you sleeping. Your hair is still gathered in its pigtails and will be all knots come morning. Your face is green and red, like Christmas, and your mouth is open. I wish we could have a lit-up ceiling all year, because the little window does not invite enough brightness. And yet in spring we will plant pansies there, that is our plan. We will add good soil to the patch of dirt now covered by snow, and from here we will see them blooming. It will not be like the garden at home, with its walls of corn and its balls of purple allium, but it will be something. The flowers will draw bees and butterflies. At night we might see moths drinking. You sleep and I look forward to that time, when the snow melts and the frost uncovers the glass and lets us see again.

There was nothing to see now but the flag. I stood as though waiting for someone to come out and then I turned and walked slowly back to College Street, where there were too many people, all of them strangers. On the pavement there was too much dog shit. Simon once told me the streets in Florence were covered with shit, though Florence in my imagination had always been perfect.

Simon had been raised in the greatest cities of the world, not in the Ottawa Valley. *G'day, G'day, I'm from the Valley.* We had pins that said that, remember? People in the city thought they read "Gee-day, Gee-day," as though it was a mysterious day of celebration. "What is Gee-day?" they asked. Simon might have read those pins that way. When we were in Paris, he gorged himself on baguettes because he said France was the only place in

the world where you could count on the bread to be perfect. It was a law, he said. He made us divine chocolate
sandwiches and I thought of the thin white sandwiches
Lucy used to make, pink baloney in-between. I remembered the dough-ball snacks we made ourselves, slowly
tearing off the crusts and wadding the bread with our
bare dirty hands. Dough-balls were chewy and moist,
turning even stale bread delicious.

I could picture Simon's past as though it were my
own, so well did I know the stories. Through him I
learned that the Leaning Tower of Pisa had 261 steps. He
had a photo of himself lying on the grass in front of it,
his chin in his little-boy's hands. Lying alone because he
was an only child. *I'm an only child, you're an only child*,
that's what he said.

I missed his bad jokes. "Chestnut," I'd say when he
told one. How hard he tried to make me laugh. He was
decent and kind, even at the very end. He was unlike
our father. Instead of raging or swearing, he told jokes.
I remembered the day Lucy left, how she had tried to
wave at Dad and how he had just stared straight ahead.
Too-big Blue was on his lap, panting and taking up all
the space between our father and the steering wheel,
but our father looked right through him. Still, he was
letting her go, a truth we could not fathom, knowing
that once when she had left in a fight he had followed
her out and dragged her back in, and that time she had

not even really been leaving, not for good anyway, just for air.

"I have another joke for you," Simon said outside the airport.

Your poor eyes look so sore, I thought, seeing the redness that must have come from crying.

"There's this man and this woman," he told me. "They've been married for years, and one night the man comes home from work and his wife's standing on the porch with her suitcase beside her. 'Where are you going?' the man asks. 'I'm leaving,' she says. 'I just found out there's this place where I can make a hundred bucks a crack doing what I've been doing with you for free all these years.' She goes to pick up her suitcase and the man says, 'Hang on!' and he rushes into the house and comes out a minute later with his own suitcase packed. 'Where do you think you're going?' asks the wife. 'I'm going with you,' he says. 'I wanna see how you can survive on four hundred bucks a year!'"

The joke was joyless, told with his fake-smiling face.

When I first met him he could make me laugh until my insides ached, not with man-made jokes but with the effortless humour that came from inside him. He called that my dulcimer laugh, pretending to be romantic, and it made us both laugh harder because my true laugh was far from gentle, it was raucous and snorting—but you know that, Eugenie, it was your laugh too.

I thought of the way I was when I met him, saw my back-then self as though from above, and saw Simon too, each of us wending our way through the people towards and away from each other. I had on my red dress with the empire waist, and later I would feel his hands there, on the high-up seam, rubbing the velvet. I saw us circle and miss, circle and miss, moving closer and closer through the people who, from above, looked now like swirls of colours, daubs of paint, props on the stage of our meeting. How easily we might have missed each other altogether.

The night he took me to the airport it was windy. It was windy all the time by then, and it rained and rained. I slipped my hand into his coat pocket and squeezed his fingers.

"You should go," I said. "Don't wait with me."

But he was not speaking. His hard shoes scuffed the pavement and wet leaves stuck to them. I removed my hand from his pocket and slid it into my own. Inside was a ball of tissue, fluffs of lint.

We crossed the parking lot and reached the entrance. Stood looking at each other. He stepped back and stood there, his arms hanging useless at his sides, and then he turned and was gone. It was both awful and a relief to see him walking away.

Then I was alone, but not truly. You were beside me. I wondered what you would say, could you speak? You never grew old enough to love someone other than me, other than Blue and Lucy and Dad. I wanted to tell you this, a thing I've known always: Light and heavy, love is not a lasting spell. It is not like sisters, where nothing is a question. You make it up as you go along. I wanted so badly to tell you that, though what possible difference could it have made for you to know?

Simon was a big surprise. I held him in too-high esteem when I first met him, because it seemed he had been everywhere and knew too many languages. It made me afraid to let him know me. And when I saw his kindness, and his own endearing faults, his love of baseball and peanut butter, by then I had lied for so long it seemed crazy. Like nothing I could ever explain.

Soon after we met, Simon seared tuna on the barbecue and I had never eaten tuna that did not come from a can. Press the lid to squeeze the liquid out. How different it looked and tasted! It lay in long slices on a bed of greens, deep pink and delicious. He had set the table with a cloth and double plates, and in the candlelight I thought I might be beautiful. Everything I said was spellbinding, astonishing me. What was it I had said? Where did I think of all those things? His easy grace did not make me awkward, but graceful too. He could rub off on me. I had felt almost dead by the time Simon found me, but with him I would be new.

The Man and the Statue

He did not know where he had been before, or even if he had existed. He did not know his name, or that he might have one. The world was blue-tinged grey and there were pigeons in it. When it was bright, dogs pulled people into the world, and when it grew dark, they pulled them out again, and he was alone. He slept on a bench and the parts of his body that touched wood were sore through the night, but the parts that touched the thin spaces between the wood were comfortable enough to make up for all that soreness, caressed as they were by air. The air was cold, but it was growing warmer. Each day the grey world took on more blue, and the white carpet folded slowly back to its dull-green underlay. The pigeons had red feet, and they shared their bread with him. He found that if he opened his hand, the people who came with dogs dropped shining coins into it, which he could trade with the man at the edge of the world for what was called real food. Real food was not what the squirrels ate; it did not grow on trees.

He began to notice things he had not noticed before.

There was a woman standing stiffly in the centre of the world, so stiffly, in fact, and so thoroughly black, that she might have been made from marble. How was it he had gone so long unaware of her? Perhaps it was the carpet of white which now drew his eye towards her. It had vanished from everywhere else but remained clumped and dirty around her feet. He walked a wide circle around her, watching her black eyes which were hard to see in the rest of her black self. He had never before seen anyone who had black where the whites of her eyes should be. He circled closer, keeping his gaze upon her. When he stood in front of her, she seemed to be looking right at him, but when he moved past, her eyes did not follow. From the side he saw that her nose was fine and straight, the nostrils with a slight triangular flare. He circled closer. She was tall but she was cheating, standing on a block of cement. Off of that, she would be as small as he. Or onto that, he would be as tall as she.

"Hello," he said.

He put forth his left hand to shake hers, and when she did not respond he drew it back and put forth his right, realizing his mistake. He had seen other people in the world do this, both with their dogs and with each other, but the woman's hands remained stiffly at her sides. Perhaps she thought he wanted coins and had nothing to give. Still she stood, as though made from stone. Yet she did not seem unfriendly. She seemed merely frozen, not unwilling but unable to speak or move or smile. He felt a surging tenderness at the thought of such an affliction.

"It will be warmer soon," he said. "I notice it's warmer each day."

A pigeon alighted on her head then, the red feet shocking against the hard black lines of her hair.

"Oh!" he said, delighted. "You have a pigeon on your head!"

And though her expression did not vary, something in it told him she felt ridiculous and that she did not enjoy feeling this way. He thought she looked divine with the pigeon there, and told her so.

"I wish they would land on me," he said. "I put my arm out for them sometimes but they just fly right by. I cannot stand so still as you—I'm jittery, you see?" He held his hand up and indeed it trembled. "Quick movement frightens them. Have you seen them fly from dogs? I think there is nothing quite as magnificent."

Still she stood.

The pigeon spread its scalloped wings and took flight, dropping upon her dignified head a runny translucent smear.

"Oh," he said.

The heat of her own shame spread through him and coloured his cheeks. He thought her proud and stoic to remain even now as she was. From the ground he fetched an oak leaf, brittle and brown, and reached towards the sullied spot. And as he touched her she came alive in colour. Shiny yellow hair sprang from her head, her black eyes filled up with white and blue, and her lips, pink now, spread into a smile.

"Oh," he said again, because she was lovelier than pigeons in flight. He held the leaf to her head and stood looking at her and she leaned forward and with her soft mouth kissed closed his left eye and then his right eye, and when he opened them she was once more black and hard and cold, staring past him.

That night he lay again on the bench. The hard slats of wood seemed harder and the narrow soothing spaces between them narrower, less soothing. He did not know the word *lonely* because he had never been anything but lonely until he touched her alive. From where he lay he could see her, glowing with the moon. He wished he could sleep with his eyes open, that he might look upon her all night long. That he might not miss it should she come alive again. When finally he closed his eyes, he felt her lips there once more and the heat of her breath warming his face.

When he woke, the sun was yawning and stretching its gold limbs, casting a slow brightness into the world. He rose and went straight to the woman. He sat at her black feet and leaned against her and held his palm open longer than normal, and when there were enough coins in his hand he took them to the man at the edge of the world and traded them for two pieces of real food.

"You're rich today!" said the man, and he said yes, he was.

*

By the end I could no longer keep track of all the lies I'd told Simon. No one had ever wanted to know me as completely as he had, but I remained unknowable. I made up a past. I modelled myself on Adele Fortier from kindergarten, remember her? She wore thin white hose when we were all still wearing leotards. All of her clothes were pastel—pale blue, pale green, pale pink—and the elastics at the ends of her braids matched each outfit. I gave myself Adele's parents and let them die tragically in a crash. I gave myself no sister. It meant there were many things I couldn't tell him.

As I wait now in Toronto, hiding from him and from home, I feel an undeniable need to tell him everything. To find a beginning, and start there, releasing the huge small story in an orderly way. Telling him, Eugenie, instead of you, because though you are always with me, you are, after all, long gone.

PART TWO **SIMON**

CHAPTER 13 **EACH OTHER**

Simon, I had a twin. When we were very small—I think four years old—we lay on the road and waited for the school bus to come. We thought it could ride right over top of us and we would come out unscathed. We lay holding sweaty hands, looking up at the moving clouds. It was September, still hot. The bare backs of our legs absorbed the heat of the newly paved road as we waited for the thrilling moment.

But we were not run over. We were not allowed the awe of being under that bus, in brief darkness, seeing the wheels turn on either side of us. Instead there were long blasts of a horn and we lifted our heads to see our father there, in the rust-scabbed car, and oh, he was angry! He opened the door and left it that way, sticking out from the rest of the car, and he walked over to where we still lay, and when we saw his red face and the muscle in his jaw moving, we stopped giggling. He grabbed our wrists and he pulled us to our feet, and he asked were we crazy, didn't we know we could have been killed? I don't remember what else he said, only that around my wrist the skin hurt, like with an Indian sunburn. We were baffled. We had never thought we might be killed. We knew the sleepy pattern of the road we lived on—that nothing drove by in the afternoons except that creeping school bus, too slow to be a danger. Still he was angry. We had never seen him so angry. He pulled us across the street and up the walk and into our house. We had to keep up with his huge strides and it was hard, walking, because one of my thongs had slid from between my toes, and when I had quickly tried to slip it on again, it had gone between the middle toes, and all I could think was how wrong it looked, how strange it felt.

Inside was Lucy. She was making a lamp for our room. A huge balloon hung suspended from fishing line, and on it she had pasted pieces of blue and green tissue paper, because blue was my favourite colour, green was my sister's.

She looked up, surprised to see us. Each tip of her finger held the gluey substance and she kept her hands open in front of her.

"What's wrong?" she asked.

That was not the right thing.

"What's wrong?!" He shook our arms and tightened his grip on our wrists. *"What's wrong?!"* He was pulling now. I thought my arm might pop out of its socket. And then suddenly he let us go and my arm flopped down by my side and as my hand hit my hip I remembered this:

We are standing in doorways, Eugenie on one side of the hall, me on the other. We hold our arms straight at our sides, but slightly raised so that the backs of our hands touch the door jamb.

"Now press," he says. "Press as hard as you can. Pretend you're trying to make the door wider."

We press. I can feel my own face reddening as I watch Eugenie's.

"Okay!" he says. "Let go!"

We each step forward, towards each other, and up float our magic weightless arms.

That was unlike now. My arm at my side felt heavy, and the skin was still burning where his hand had been. I peered around him to my sister and saw her looking at the wall. I tried looking there too, to see if it might be like nothing was happening, but I could not help looking back. I could not help seeing his hand swing out to hit the patchy balloon, and though the sound of it popping was loud and shocking, the sight of it vanished in the blink of an eye.

Down his back were four white lines of glue, fine trails left by Lucy's fingers as she reached too late to stop him.

Later we were in our room. It was candyfloss pink then, not the underwater blue and green it would soon become. The shouting went on and on. My sister lay on her bunk and looked through a picture book.

From the window I could see the car, still there in the road with its door hanging open. There was the faint sound of the radio coming from within, a voice singing to no one.

This was like a summer night, hot, still and dry, but it was not summer any more. September was deceiving. Soon the leaves would turn and fall and then would be the bare cold time before winter. This bush right here, the lilac tree, soon it would look like a twig. There would not be the thickly sweet blooms again until May, maybe June, a long time to wait for that fragrance. A lilac's leaves were strange and almost veinless, like a finger without prints.

Not until the sun sank low did he go to move the car. I watched him from the window, hiding behind the curtain. I wanted to see what he looked like now that he was different, now that we all were.

But the streetlight shone down on him, showing him just the same. His same curling hair, glossy brown, his same navy sweater now marred by glue. His shoulders which he always held straight and broad, his so-long legs climbing into the car. There was nothing different about him, and so maybe there was nothing different about any of us. I knew, watching him, that he would park the car in its same spot on the driveway, covering the oil stains, and when he came in he would close the screen door quietly and all would be silent in the house, no yelling, no sobbing. Soon the television would come on, bringing the familiar sound of strangers' voices, of canned laughter, and that fight would be as though it never had been.

I knew that later she would slip into our room and kiss us each one and whisper, *He loves you, is all, he just loves you so much.* We didn't yet know how many times we would hear those words. She would lie on the loveseat and tell stories until we were sound asleep, and then she would sleep too, having lulled herself. Sleep where she was in our room with her head bent forward and her braids still in and we would all sleep dreaming, *He loves you, is all. He just loves you so much.*

It always seemed to come from nowhere. We didn't know when to expect it, what to expect. Or I didn't. I could never accept it was him, behaving that way. That it had settled in as a regular part of what made my father. Every time I saw it, it seemed like a rare thing, one of the first times, as though I had never seen the violent vein in his temple, as though it was a big surprise.

Never before had we seen him so angry.

But we had. We had seen it switch off and on all our lives. So when I search for the beginning, I search for that very first time things went wrong, but now I wonder, Did it start before me?

Inside their bedroom was a hole in the wall that had always been there. I knew it had been made by the doorknob because I had many times pushed the door back as far as it would go and I had seen that the knob fit the hole, which was ragged around the edges, as though the wall was made from cardboard. I did not know how it had happened, why a door might be swung so hard, but I knew it made me sick to see it. Looking through showed me nothing but another wall. My sister sometimes dropped food in there, to feed the beings we could not see.

CHAPTER 14 SHE, LIKE ME

Lucy's birthday is February 29th, a day that does not always exist, so we celebrate on the 28th. Had it been a leap year that winter, everything may have been different. Lucy's birthday would have fallen on a Friday. Instead it did not come at all. The last day of February was a Thursday, the night Lucy now took a clay-modelling course. Not long after our father's visit, she was rejuvenated by the constant presence of Camille Claudel and *La Valse*. Whenever she told us the tragic story of Camille ending up in the madhouse, she would add, "You should know how lucky we are to live in this age. These are the nineteen-eighties. We can be whoever we want to be."

Because it was Thursday, and not a leap year, Lucy was not home when our father came smiling to surprise her. He had in his hands a wrapped present and he stood holding it as the smile washed from his face.

He was angry to know she was out, had left us alone. Shocked to see us wearing her bright lipstick, blue shadow on our eyelids. My sister had borrowed her second-hand clothes, but I could never do that. No matter how many times they were washed, they did not smell clean or like us but like someone we didn't know, and also like must, like damp basements. I could see stains on them. Yellow crescent armpits, a see-through splotch of grease.

We were getting so much older, that is what he must have thought. He dropped the present and took my sister's face in his hands, and with his big thumbs he smudged the outline of blue around her eyes. He said we looked like sluts. He did not know it was only dress-up, only play, and because of his mood we did not say.

He told us we had to come with him. He swung wide the closet door and he rummaged through the things in there, cramming clothes into the floral canvas suitcases we'd arrived with. He did not know whose was whose, what was what. A blouse of Lucy's was caught in the zipper. I felt so sad for him. I saw the anger in my sister's made-up eyes as she watched him. She did not take her eyes from him, even when he looked at her.

"We're not going," she said.

And he grabbed her wrist like he had done before and he said, "Yes, you are."

All she did was stare.

"We should wait for Lucy," I said. "At least until she gets here."

We had made an easy-bake cake and decorated it with jelly beans. It was waiting for her on the counter.

"Fuck her," he said.

There was a long empty silence, and then he laughed and went kind to cover his blunder. He could not mean such a thing, not ever. I saw that in his face, in the dimples that showed when he smiled. Now he was back again, the good him. He took his hand from my sister's wrist and ran it through her hair. And then he turned and put his arms around me and he picked me up. I was light as air, a paper doll.

"I want you to come home," he said into my ear. "I want you all home." His breath was hot, the smell of grief in it.

Eugenie came because I did. She did not say one word. We sat in the back seat together and watched the city going by. We were in a sea of blurry lights from buildings, from cars, and snow was coming down. All along the sidewalks people were hurrying, or gathered in shelters waiting for streetcars to come. Our father swore and pressed on the horn. The wipers spread back and forth on the windshield, pushing the snow away. It took a long time to leave the city, which sprawled and sprawled, and after it was gone there was only the pure white of snow. White roads, white meadows, white trees against a black liquid sky. I could not find the moon. And the snow that fell became hail and then sleet, a wall through which we could not see.

He was driving too fast. The tickle-hills that had once been thrilling to drive over, turning our stomachs, were not thrilling now. I thought I would be sick, and I wondered how angry that would make him. I looked at my sister but her face was turned away to the window, and so I turned to my own window, to the blur of white. I pressed my face against the cold glass and hoped for no more hills.

How long had my eyes been closed when I heard her?

"Slow down," she said.

She sounded like someone I did not know. A grown-up stranger.

"Slow down," she said again.

I could feel the car swerving. I kept my eyes closed and I heard her unclasp her seat belt, the click of it opening, and then I felt her hand on my thigh, a nail digging in, as she leaned between the bucket seats to tell him again.

When he braked I lurched forward but the belt held me. I opened my eyes and saw her coat billow, her boots in the air. My hands stretched out after her as she flew through the glass.

That arm that had once been broken, it was broken again, bent at an impossible angle that made my own arm ache. I remembered the time I had fallen from the tree, landing my heavy self upon my sister's body, feeling her heartbeat there. Now her heart had stopped. I did not have to touch her to know. I saw her lying in the snow, an angel face-down, and I saw more snow gather upon her, in her hair and on her coat, in the folds of her used, borrowed clothes.

For all the noise that the crashing glass had made, now there was near-silence. The engine had stopped but the headlights were on. Through the hole where the windshield had been I watched snowflakes fall in the yellow beam of light. Cold came in through the opened space. The smallest snowflakes found me all the way in the back seat, where I sat still with my belt on. They floated in and touched my face and melted. On and off I heard a flapping sound, driven by wind. It sounded to me like summer shoes on pavement, two steps, three steps, nothing. The snow kept falling. The wind rose again and I saw what made the sound: a visor hanging, knocking against the window frame.

With me in the car was my father. Leaning forward, slumped on the wheel. They would call the fluid they dripped into his arm a solution, but it would not be that. In the end there would be him and me and Lucy, all that was left. I would go to school and come home, go to school and come home, waiting only for the day I would not have to come home any more. And then, wherever I might be, there would be only me.

CHAPTER 15 OVER AND OVER

I wonder what you are doing now, Simon. If it is warm there, and windy, and if you are thinking of me. I wish right now to be sharing custard with you, the way you make it with jam blobbed in the middle. If you knew what I've been eating, you'd be appalled. But I was raised on fish sticks, I can tell you that now, though I suppose you've always suspected.

Do you know how much I miss you, and how sorry I am? There were times I thought about nothing other than telling you. I analysed when and how I could do it. I went over and over it in my mind, making new versions of how it would be, just as I've gone over and over the death of my sister. Willing a new conclusion. That was what Millicent did: lived and relived the ugly part until she could make a difference, until the story unfolded just the way she wished. You drew her perfectly, with her long white feet and plain face. What amazed and frightened me most was your surprising intuition as to how each character should look and act. And though you disliked Millicent, you drew her. You said she was too much like Ildikoh, with her horns and her extrasensory perception. And when I asked you what was wrong with telling an old story a new way, you shrugged and said that there was whimsy missing from Millicent, that the story was relentlessly sad. I told you that some stories are, that I had wanted it that way, and after that you simply drew the sadness in. You made the images small and plain, with lots of white space around them. You used colour sparingly—for the figs and the berries, for the speeding yellow car—so the brightness shocked when it suddenly showed on a page.

MILLICENT
AND THE THOUSAND PENNIES

Millicent's bones were mysterious. They held her together in all the regular ways, but down her back they formed a spine of horns. Together with this, she had the uncontrollable ability to see flashes of the past and future. Which was the gift and which the affliction, she knew not, for each trait was so extraordinary that one could not be separated from the other. She had never been without the stegosaurus horns, so she knew not the easy comfort of a regular spine. Her own seemed no hardship and no boon, yet the visions, at times, could be either. For instance, years after her actual birth had taken place, Millicent saw herself born again, as though for the first time. A woman groaned and pushed and a bony creature emerged. The warm wet darkness was replaced by a bright cold world and the slithering lifeline that might pull her back in was cut and knotted. What happened to the woman Millicent did not know, for she had not seen her before or since, but she missed her.

As a child, Millicent was passed from home to home, yet she may as well have grown up alone, like Tarzan, eating nuts and berries. Sometimes she was told to quit whining—"The woman you miss so much ran screaming at the sight of you." Other times she was told no use crying—"The woman you pine for was split in two by the very birth of you." Either way, Millicent's fault.

When she grew up she left everyone behind, but her greatest wish remained, which was to relive the moment of her birth, to go back in and come out smooth and normal, or perhaps not emerge at all. Imagine if life went backward, she thought. What might become of us?

She was mulling such a question when she saw a boy killed by a speeding yellow car. Then she saw it again. So vivid were the images, she was unsure which was the most real, the premonition or its fulfilment.

You should have seen her eyes that day. The whole awful scene was reflected in them, and coloured hazel. She had first searched to find him. She ran barefoot on the burning black road. It was blistering August, a Thursday afternoon. She ran so fast, so hard, the seam of her dress split and her left leg flashed out. She arrived in time only to shout out and see the boy killed anyway, exactly the way he had been killed the first time. His tiny slip-on shoe, a sandal, flying through the air.

What was most horrible was that she recognized him as the well-loved boy she saw often at market, ambling with his mother and father. The mother and father now stooped and cried beside the boy's bleeding body. Millicent watched their sobbing backs. The mother laid down with her son but the father stood up and looked at the gathering crowd. His face was drained of colour except for the red crying eyes.

Millicent could not look at him. She lowered her eyes from his sorrow and looked at her feet. She was woozy with déjà vu, and all the while she was heaving, short of breath. She had run so far, she thought she may as well keep going. She walked and walked. She didn't bring anything with her. She had her bare feet, which once had been all people needed, and her mesh bag, fruitless and hanging from her wrist.

The thing was, she had been heading to that very corner anyway, to buy fruit. She had collected her mesh bag, her hat and her change purse. She had put on her shoes. She had pushed the door open and stepped out and then the dead heat of August engulfed her. Instead of following the path to the street, she cut across the lawn to the shaded relief of the willow tree. She slipped off her shoes and climbed into the hammock. A monarch fluttered by. She dozed, but a chirping bird, a grosbeak, kept rousing her. There was no awful feeling. A breeze washed in, exquisitely cooling. The willow leaves touched each other. The long, arching branches swayed and the hammock swayed too, and Millicent, swaying, savoured the luxury of lying on her back, a thing she could not do in a regular bed.

His body flew and landed and his shoe kept flying. The instant she saw him she was up and running, still asleep in a way, but flying too, too late. A sound came out of her mouth and went unheard because of another sound, metallic, and there was his shoe again. There was no weight to him any more, nothing to hold that shoe on, and yet he was heavy, dead weight when they lifted him from the road, dead weight in her memory.

The boy's father and mother ran to the well-loved son and kneeled over him; they gently shook his arm and touched his face, but it was seconds too late, far, far too late. Millicent closed her eyes to the desolation, and when she opened them, the boy's father was running frantically from person to person, as though something could still be done. He grabbed Millicent's elbow and turned her so that she was looking into his bloodless face.

"Help," he cried. "Please help us." His open mouth a dark hole.

The boy's name had been Martin Neil, or Neil Martin, she could never remember, and the shame of that meant she could never speak of him out loud, which she longed to do, that he would not be lost completely. Without a name he might become any faceless boy, and he was not any boy, he was Martin or Neil, well loved. A specific boy with specific blond hair parted on the left, specific shoes which were two-strap sandals, cuffed specific shorts and specific socks rolled at the ankles. Such was the responsibility she felt that every detail should have been indisputable. But it wasn't.

Not even the boy's father saw her leave. And if anyone had, they would never have guessed she was leaving completely. Not with her bare feet and her empty bag. Her hat and her change purse, containing just enough to buy fruit, still lay on the grass beneath the hammock, and the hammock itself was still swinging, so violently had she risen upon seeing that vision. The grosbeak had long gone, and the butterfly had gone and returned, gone and returned, because that was the way of butterflies. By the time Millicent had reached the next town, by bare burning foot, the butterfly had left the scene of the accident (the premonitory scene, that is) 114 times, and returned as many. All that was left where the body had been was the dark stain of blood, looking no different than a stain from leaking oil.

That had been a windy day. At some points, the wind rose to hurricane proportions and then eerily died again. A loose tile on the roof of Millicent's ramshackle house flap-flapped and kept Millicent from dozing as she lay in her hammock. The hammock swayed, even swung, and the fluttering butterfly kept trying to land on the willow's weeping branches, but over and over the wind got under its wings and lifted it up and away. A little victim of circumstance. The grosbeak, barrel-chested, folded its wings and clenched its toes and hung on.

How could it have been so hot if it was so windy?

In any case, it was August, a Thursday afternoon. The wind brought paltry relief from the stifling heat because it was just air of the same scalding temperature blowing around and stirring everything up. In the sky there was no window that could be opened to lessen the heat of the day. Millicent felt unsettled. Or too settled. Something was wrong. She could not get comfortable. This beloved hammock may as well have been a flat horrid bed, for the bones of her spine landed each on a knot, not a space, when she first lay down. The grosbeak would not shut up. It chirped and chirped, and when she glared up at it, it blinked and opened its mouth and chirped again. Something was wrong. Grosbeaks travelled in groups. She knew this because just last week five of them had flown smack into her picture window and dropped to their deaths in the garden. There had been blood on the window, and a single feather stuck there, slithering down. Millicent had stood looking at the clean pane of glass and then she'd seen it all again. Now she thought of their five broken necks. They travel in groups, no matter what. She looked up at the squawking solitary bird, into its unblinking eye, and that was when she saw Martin, or Neil, a gust of wind lifting him right off his small sandalled feet and Millicent, too, flew, but her mesh bag, which hung from her waist, got tangled in the mesh of the hammock, and in her frenzy to pull these apart her dress ripped at the waist and a flash of her stomach appeared. She ran and ran. Too late, she called out. He was hit and lifted again into the air. The wind held him, and then stopped when he landed. There was not even a breeze. The only air came from the gasping mouths of the onlookers. Millicent stood with her hot hands on her hot face. Through her fingers she watched the mother and father crouch beside their well-loved boy.

There was a loud howling cry, which Millicent at first thought came from the mother, but no, it had not, for the mother was serene, surreal, lying down beside her son and whispering into his unhearing ear. The cry had come from Millicent herself. She knew because now the boy's father had appeared at her elbow, telling her, "Ssshhh," and stroking her hair, as though she were the one who needed comforting.

"You couldn't have seen it coming," he said.

But she could have, and did.

She was shaking all over. The sweat that had formed as she ran was now chilling. She was cold in her bones. She thought of her birth and the way the woman's hair had spread like yellow waves across the pillow. She crossed her arms and hugged herself, walked away from the scene and kept walking, though she knew not where or why. Her feet were bare, but she did not care. Nor did she care about her ripped dress or her missing hat, though the sun was strong and she was prone to sunstroke. Her change purse was back by the hammock. It had flown when she had, up into the air, all the coins spilling out and landing like glinting stars in the grass. Her mesh bag was with her, meant to be stretched full with fruit. Empty, it hung from her torn waistband. Anyway she could not eat. How would she ever eat again, knowing she had failed him? She saw his little arms, how they rose and

crossed and covered his face. Behind him was the fruit stand.
Heaps of soft blushing mangoes and papayas piled up. She
would have held the fruit in her hand and smelled it.

She had made a list:

mango
strawberries
cantaloupe
bananas
papaya (2?)

because although it was expensive, it was her undeniable
favourite. She tucked the list into her change purse, stepped
into her sandals and grabbed her hat, which hung from a hook
by the door. She pushed the door open and stepped outside
and then the dead heat of August engulfed her, and all she
wanted was to lie still in the hammock with her eyes closed.
She almost did that. She almost crossed the lawn and kicked
off her sandals and lay dozing in the shade. She stood on the
porch, looking over at the tree. There was a bird there, chirp-
chirping, and a wandering monarch unable to land. She took
a step towards the hammock and just then a gust of wind
came up, so strong it blew the hat from her head and she ran
chasing it and laughing, because each time she almost had it,
it touched the ground and was lifted again, far out of reach.
The flap-flap of a loose tile on the roof of Millicent's ramshackle house matched the slap of her sandals as she lurched

after the hat. All the way she did that. She arrived at the fruit stand hatless. Short of breath, she stood beside the mound of mangoes and the hat flew on without her. And then all she did was gather fruit. In her mesh bag she placed the mango and then a basket of strawberries, but what she did not know was that the basket had flipped over, and strawberries were dropping out from the holes in the bag. That was the trouble with mesh. Or strawberries, depending on how you looked at it. She might have lost all of them, were it not for Martin or Neil. He tapped her elbow and she turned. There he stood with his cupped hands full of berries. He had blond hair parted neatly on the right. His crisp shirt was buttoned all the way up to his neck, though it was too hot for that, and she had a strange urge to unbutton it, to blow with her breath inside it, which of course she did not do.

"These are yours," he said.

"Oh!" she said. "Thank you." And she stooped and opened her bag, refilling the basket. When she looked up, she caught him staring at her back. Her dress was open there, specially tailored for a spine with horns.

"Are you an animal?" he asked.

Millicent smiled. It was an innocent question, asked only because he didn't know.

"My name is Millicent," she told him. "What's your name?"

"Martin," he answered. And then, "Neil."

(Afterwards she thought about that part repeatedly, because surely it meant that his given name was Martin. Was that not what he had said? But he was such a strange and stiff little fellow, too proper with his cuffed shorts and his tidy rolled socks. Socks in sandals! She'd thought immediately upon hearing him, with only this as evidence, that he had silently inserted a comma, making his name Martin, Neil, and so Neil Martin.)

"Thank you," she said again. She handed him a strawberry, stood and walked away. And it was not until she was waiting in line that she saw him again. She looked up at the large round mirror meant to trap shoplifters, and there he was in mid-air. She pushed past the people and raced out through the doors with her stretched bag of stolen fruit, and she might have made it in time had it not been for her sandal, whose sole had come loose and flap-flapped, causing her to trip and fly, shouting out as she landed, but the shout was lost in the shrill squeal of tires on pavement, and emitted too late.

She stayed where she was. She did not want to look up. She had scraped her elbow and it stung even more when a man's hand wrapped around it.

"Good God, lady, what are you trying to do?"

Millicent looked past him and out into the street. She could see the hunched figures of the mother and father, and just then the father's eyes met hers. Dark eyes in a sallow grieving face. Millicent looked away. Far off the strawberry rolled, whole and unharmed. She thought of the day of her birth, and the unmoving hair, yellow against the white pillow, and the well-loved boy who had died. It was time to start walking, but where? She had never been to the next town, and only vaguely knew the way.

Still, that was where she'd been headed this morning. She had heard there was water there, and a long white rockless beach. And hadn't she had a map, a piece of paper tucked into her change purse? Yes. She had gathered her hat and her change purse, containing the map and also enough money for fruit. She searched and searched for her mesh bag, but it was not to be found, so she left the house without it. It was blistering August, a Thursday afternoon. The heat was so stifling that not even the fierce random wind brought any lasting relief. A day like this could sap the life from a body if a body failed to treat itself with the utmost care. For this reason, she planned to bring her hammock. Not only could she happily loll in it at the beach, she could fold and fold it until it was like her mesh bag, and she could fill it with fruit for her sojourn. With this plan, she stepped out into the day's thick heat and approached the weeping willow. On one of the hooks that held the hammock to the tree, there was a butterfly resting, and on the other, a bird, and when she shooed them away to unhook the hammock, she had a feeling more chilling than déjà vu. The butterfly fluttered and the bird, a grosbeak, flapped and squawked. It held its feet out and spread its skinny grey toes. She could see only blackness in its flashing liquid eyes, and then four more birds swooped in with a gust of wind and this fifth was carried off among them. Millicent stood for a moment, willing the awful feeling away. The wind died as she folded the hammock, and then it blew in again, sending the butterfly flying and her hat, too, flying wingless without her. She ran chasing her hat and laughing, because each time she almost had it, it touched the ground and was lifted again, far out of reach. The slap-slap of a loose tile on the roof of Millicent's ramshackle house matched the flap of the butterfly's wings, so it seemed the paper-thin monarch was making all that racket alone. Millicent ran and ran, and was too far away from home to be hearing the tile, and yet the noise persisted. Breathless, astonished, she stopped, and the noise stopped too. She looked down at her sandalled feet and up at the monarch and her hat, disappearing in silence.

And then all she did was gather fruit. In her hammock-cum-bag, she placed two papayas, her undeniable favourite, then a basket of blue figs, but what she did not know was that the basket had flipped over and the figs were dropping out of the too-big holes. That was the trouble with hammocks. Or with figs, depending on how you looked at it. All the while her load got lighter. She might have lost everything were it not for Martin or Neil. He tapped her elbow and she turned. There he stood with his cupped hands full of figs. He had blond hair neatly parted on the left. His crisp shirt was buttoned all the way up to his neck, though it was too hot for that today. Sweat darkened his collar and the roots of his hair. His round face was flushed pink, a sign of the blood pumping through him.

"You dropped these," he said.

"Oh!" she said. "Thank you." And when she stooped to refill her basket, she caught him staring at her back, where her dress hung open, specially tailored for a spine with horns.

He flushed more deeply, ashamed to have been caught. But still he asked, needing to know.

"Are you an animal?"

"Yes," she told him.

He blinked. Sweat trickled from his temple.

Millicent smiled and leaned forward. "I'm a dinosaur," she whispered. She put her hand on his face, undid the top button of his collar and blew on his suffering neck. "We're not extinct after all, you see." She stepped back and looked at him. "And who are you?" she asked.

"My name is Martin," he told her. "Martin Neil."

She pulled a fig from her bag, blew the dirt from it and popped it in the mouth of Martin Neil.

After that she didn't even think of him until she was waiting in line to pay for her fruit. He was just a regular boy, after all. She had touched his hot face and nothing had made her afraid for him, and she was often frightened for people when she saw into them. So she stood in line and looked up into the concave mirror and found herself there, among strangers, and then she saw Martin, flying. She pushed past the people with her folded hammock full of fruit and she ran, flew, to save him, out through the doors and onto the street where, oh, he is standing.

He is standing on the other side of the street. There is no wind, and it is not like before. It is hot, yes, but different. She stands looking at Martin Neil in his tiny pleated shorts and his sandals, fastened firmly with buckles. Cars pass between them. He looks right at her and just at that moment a rough hand grabs Millicent's elbow.

"You pay for that stuff?" asks the man.

"No, but—"

This is when the wind comes. Martin is blown forward, light as paper, and Millicent has to strain against the wind to get to him in time. She opens her mouth and the sound that comes out is squealing tires. She sees his arms rise and cross and cover his face and she grabs him by the wrists, pushing him back. His wrists are so small. Of course she is frightened. Her body flies and lands and her sandals keep flying. The air is nice on the whole naked surface of her feet. The pennies from her purse have flown up into the sky and now are raining down with her. Enough pennies to pay for everything. She closes her eyes and thinks about her unharmed feet in the white sand, in the see-through water. About swimming yellow hair.

CHAPTER 16 BISECTED

After the accident my father lay in a hospital bed which could be adjusted by means of a button. On his forehead was a gash stitched in black. The little knots that held the stitches in place made me think of sewing, which Lucy had tried and tried to teach us, but we had not been open to learning. Now there were millions of things Eugenie would not ever come to know.

I sat in a chair in a corner of my father's room, which was grey-white, as was outside. The dull light of morning made the window like another painted wall. I wanted to touch the stitches on my father's face, but I did not want to touch my father. The gash was from where his head had hit the steering wheel. I knew because I had seen him resting there. I had thought for a moment he might be dead. It would have been better. To love and to miss him, mourn that loss. Instead he had lived. I had leaned forward and seen his shoulders rise and fall and known that breath and sorrow moved through him.

He had punctured a lung. It made laughing and sobbing painful, which was perhaps why he did neither. It was not an injury I could see, and so I focused on the gash and the tiny black knots. I wished for my own gash with stitches to touch. I had nothing. Not a bruise or a broken bone. They said when they examined me that I was a lucky girl.

Lucy and I spent hours just sitting with him. Sometimes I was sure we'd breathed all the air in the room, that the only air left was each other's. But I did not wish to be elsewhere. I did not yet feel restless or sore. I had no desire even to move or to sleep. I wanted only to sit and wish time backwards, turning the past present again.

All night I had replayed the accident in my mind. It could not be called a crash because there was nothing loud about it. It was a slow, quiet movement that matched the falling snow. I kept it that way in the new versions I made, but I gave myself and my father more cuts and broken bones to lift the full load of pain from Eugenie, and I put my mother in the passenger seat, turning the drive into our search for a Christmas tree. With my eyes closed I saw my sister stir in the snow.

The headlights illuminated her. As she pushed herself up with her arms the snow fell from where it had collected in the folds of her clothes. She was on her knees now, facing the trees, which were black against a black sky. I saw her take a deep breath and blow it back out again, breath that showed in a cloud, appearing and disappearing as quickly. She turned so slowly, stepping with her knees, holding her arms out at each side for balance or for fun. Her hat was askew but her face, it was perfect.

"Owww," she said, giggling.

She looked at us and laughed, as though that ride through the window had been the ride of her life, and then she stood and walked to a fresh plain of snow and fell back into it. I felt the ice cold that trickled onto her wrists and into her boots and down inside the collar of her jacket as she spread her double wings.

"Come," said my mother.

The window showed a change in the brightness of the sky, though it was still without blue. I felt I had been sleeping for a very long time. Every bone and even my skin was sore.

"Come," she said again.

She fastened all the buttons of my coat to the neck and lifted me out of the chair. I was a boneless rag doll. With ease she carried me in her long thin arms as though I were a baby. I pressed my face into the white silk of her neck.

"My skin is sore," I whispered.

"I know," she said. I felt her face against mine move into a smile. "Mine too."

I did not look at my father as we left the room. Not at his face with its stitches, nor at his long body covered by a blanket of white. I did not look at that hanging bag, filled with the solution, and not at the clear plastic tube and not at the needle that disappeared into the raised blue vein of his hand.

Lucy opened the door to our home underground. With her hand at my back she urged me inside. I saw that Eugenie's socks were still there on the floor, two little balls of cotton. Too soft, they were, stretched from all the times she'd worn them. I held them one in each palm and felt my hands fill up with the loss of her. I thought it must be true about those psychics who could hold a belonging and know the spirit of the owner.

Instead of sitting in a chair, I lay in my bed with Eugenie's empty bed beside me. I kept my clothes and boots on. Anyway, my nightgowns were packed. Stuffed into that suitcase which was in the trunk of his old jalopy which was I knew not where. Lucy lay down beside me and together we looked at the ceiling, where we had never hung the pulleys to suspend our beds. I thought with certainty that Lucy was thinking the very same thing, of Emily Carr and Eugenie, for it was then that she began to shake all over. Her long hair and her entire body trembled. Her teeth chattered. I wanted to help, to hug her, but all I could do was fold my hand into hers. She squeezed hard. She cried in a way I have not heard a person cry, not since or before, like an animal. I liked the feeling of her hurting my hand, the flexible bones bending.

Afterwards she lay looking at my profile, stroking my hair. She said, "I don't know what to do now, Janie." And I realized at that moment that we would go back to him. Just as we as a family were now broken beyond repair, Lucy was broken too, not only as a mother but in a way that had nothing to do with us. All that had come out of her quest was disaster. I kept my eyes on the ceiling and didn't respond. The truth was I didn't know what I wanted— or rather that there was nothing I wanted. I didn't want to live on, here, with Lucy and without Eugenie, and I didn't want to go home with him, where I had never been without my sister. No, there was nothing at all that I wanted, which was so different from the way I'd felt the day before. Ever since Lucy had left for Toronto, I had known exactly what I wanted: to have my whole family together.

Lucy kissed my cheek and got up from the bed. I heard her run a bath and smelled the bubbles, a green-apple smell that smelled like her. She bathed when she was sad, had always said that stepping out clean gave her the feeling of having started the day over. I, by now, had tired of living this day over, knowing it would turn out the same. And I could not imagine bathing, the energy it would take. I could not imagine moving. It was hard enough to lift my head and so I did not even do that. But if I opened my eyes, I could see my boots. They flopped away from each other like open brown wings. They leaked brown stains on the bedspread, pastel pink, brought from home.

We were six when we slept with our boots on. They were the first ones we'd owned that had zippers. Eugenie's were purple and mine were red. They were not leather but vinyl, a difference we did not see. We wore them home from the store though there was no snow, only fallen leaves on the ground. All afternoon we were go-go girls. Lucy pushed the couch and the chairs together and made a stage for us, and the places they'd been showed in worn spots on the carpet. We danced to the wrong kind of music, country, and we swivelled our hips. We sang hard into pretend microphones, and that was when he came in, to see us standing on the furniture with boots on. We froze and looked for the vein in his forehead or his fingers stretch-clenching. Instead we saw his smile.

"Pretty silly colours," he said.

But they were fake-fur lined, with red and with purple. We unzipped and showed him the warmth they

contained, and something, maybe that, made him happy.
He said he knew all the music that was best for dancing,
and of the lyrics he knew every word. He showed us how
to jive and sent us spinning, and even when we stopped,
the room did not. It was as though we stood on moving
water. He showed us the twist and how he could get right
to the ground without falling, which we could not ever
hope to do. He showed us the Charleston, his hands on
his knees, and it had to be magic that his limbs could
turn to long bands of rubber that way. Though rubber
was what our whole bodies had become. We were dizzy
with dance and with laughter.

"Okay," he said, puffing. "Sit." He gave us each a
light push and we fell back into the plush cushions of the
chesterfield. "Watch closely."

He lowered the needle to one special song and
when the music began he pulled Lucy from her chair.
She was already smiling, getting lost in him. He held
an arm at her waist and her hand in his. We could tell
by the one-two-three beat they were waltzing, though
years would pass before we knew of *La Valse*, of
Camille Claudel. With every sweeping turn Lucy's hair
swung out in a marigold spray. They pressed their
noses together and looked eye to eye until the long
song ended.

We sat watching in our hot new boots, and once it
came to be night we still did not wish to remove them.

"So don't," he said.

That was the lovely way he could sometimes be.

And yet I dreamed that in my sleep my feet grew very large. The pain was enormous because of him pressing his thumb on the toe of my boot.

"You should've got a size larger," he said to Lucy in that voice he had, with meanness.

I dreamed that as I woke I saw the little stitches splitting one by one, the beautiful fake red leather falling away.

Now in our underground home my boots were brown with brown stains beside. I tried to move my heavy feet but could not. The golden light of evening pressed on the window, proving that nearly one day had passed. I wondered if the whole rest of my life would move this slowly. I wanted to be outside, where, though there was snow, it might be warmer. But I could not move my feet or my head. That is my earliest memory of a desire that has chased me ever since. When I am here, I want to be there.

Right now I am in Toronto, and I want more than anything to be in Vancouver with you, Simon, to hear you tell again the story that Plato told, because this time I would listen more carefully. You couldn't have known when you told it how much it had sounded like one of

Lucy's stories, how it made me long for her and my sister, and even for him. I wish now to lie back and hear your voice in my ears, to hear the story the way you had intended, a story of me and of you.

We had just come from a movie, remember?

It was cool out, and raining, the way it always is there in the winter. Chilled to the bone we were, our socks soaked through. You ran me a bath and the oil smelled of jasmine, hot places. I lay immersed in the water, almost sleeping, but you kept coming in with candles until the whole room glowed clementine like another room I knew. Then you stood smiling, peeling off your damp clothes.

"No!" I said, laughing as you climbed in. "There's not enough room for two!"

But you sank down anyway and the water sloshed over the rim.

"We're not two," you said. "We're one."

All I did was roll my eyes.

"Don't you know that story?"

"No," I said. "But I'm assuming I will."

This is what you told.

Once each one of us was two. Imagine us. Whole, we have a perfect-circle body. From it grows our shared long neck and our head. Our two identical faces look in opposite directions, so that we may never miss any exquisite sight. Because we are one, we can see through each other's eyes. We have four arms and four legs and effortlessly we move this way or that without turning. It is as though we are always dancing. When we need to move quickly, we spin in reeling cartwheels. We are one mighty being and we know it. What we want most is to climb to heaven, to conquer the world and rule the formidable earth and sky. United, we are in a constant state of exhilaration. Perhaps we are too full of ourselves. We don't think so, but that is what the gods think. They are wary of our power. Jealous, perhaps, of our circular beauty. They want to keep their divine thumbs upon us, and for that they must make us weaker, half as strong.

It is for this we are split in two. Like an egg that is cut with a hair, as easily as that we are bisected. The gods turn our faces to our wounded sides, so that we may always be aware of something missing. Our skin they gather and smooth and tie at the navel, a wrinkled imperfection to remind us.

Severed, we live always longing for the day we will find our other half. It is why, when we meet, we wrap around each other the way we do. A wish that we might grow together again.

You splashed me when you finished. I, listening, had almost forgotten your presence, which seemed impossible now that I saw you again. You were big. You were taking up too much room. Your legs were wrapped around me and your knees poked up out of the water. For fun you pressed your feet into my armpits. But I was growing cold and you were leaning up against the taps, so we could not add hot water. I only wanted out. The colour of the candlelit room was too close to the colour of that other room.

"You make me so claustrophobic sometimes," I said, trying to sound light and teasing. But I was shivering now, and I was very deeply sad.

That was why you slept with your finger there, in my belly button, hoping to reconnect us. Somehow you knew of my sorrow.

Lucy emerged from the bathroom in her robe and slippers. The skin around her bloodshot eyes was raw and swollen. She sat next to me on the bed and pulled my boots off.

"I'll find you some jammies," she said. "You'll feel so much better once you're all cozied up."

I knew I would not. From here I could see that the top drawer of the dresser was askew. In his rush he had not taken care to close it properly. I did not want to go near anything he'd touched.

"I want to sleep in my clothes," I said.

"Okay." Lucy pulled my socks off and rubbed my feet with her bath-warmed hands. "Keeping your coat on too?"

I nodded.

Lucy lay beside me on the bed once more and put her hand on mine. For some time we stayed that way, and then I asked, "Where is she?" I wanted to know, was she in a long metal box, a drawer that could be opened? I thought of Uncle William's birds, their telltale paper anklets.

Lucy did not directly answer. She said it was not a body but a spirit that mattered, in life and in death. Eugenie's spirit had been loosed from her body, Lucy said, and now she was like a bird or an angel, something with wings, which gave her the ability to go everywhere. Because of that, Eugenie would always be with us, no matter where we were.

And yet, I had seen my unmoving sister in the snow. I had not lifted my eyes from her until they'd closed the doors of the ambulance and taken her away. Nothing had risen from her body.

"You can't see a soul," said Lucy. "But that doesn't mean it's not there."

I found it hard, suddenly, to believe in what I could not see.

When I awoke it was some time late into the night. The only light coming in through the window was artificial street-lamp light, and it was in this barely perceptible glow that I watched Lucy.

"Genie's going to be cremated," she said. "Do you know what that means?"

I blinked and looked at the window, at my boots, and once again at Lucy. "Burned," I said.

Lucy closed her eyes. She waited such a long time to open them that I thought she must be sleeping.

"We want to bring her home," she said, "and scatter her ashes some place special, a place that meant something to her."

I wondered why, what difference it could make, given what Lucy had said about souls. If Eugenie was already gone from her body, was she not even more gone from the ashes that would form when we burned her? But I did not ask. I said nothing.

Lucy looked at me and smiled. She pressed my nose with the tip of her finger.

"You could choose the place," she said.

She snuggled into me and began to cry in silence. I could feel her tears on the top of my head.

"I am so, so sorry," she whispered. "I never should have brought us here, should I?"

Yes, no, maybe so. How would I, ten years old, know the answer to such a question?

Sleeping, I dreamed of the licking flames, me on a teepee pyre, almost burning. No light had ever been as bright as this, no heat so hot. I was in corduroy pants and my rag-rug sweater, made from Grandma Ingrams' leftover wool, and what I was thinking was, Oh, I wish I wish I had worn my swimsuit. I was hot, and the flames were all around me, but I was not burning. And I was fine and calm until a frantic pair of hands reached through the fire, trying to touch me. Appearing, disappearing at my feet and arms and face, blind hands, aching to find me. I was calling but the roar of the fire swallowed my voice. I was reaching, grabbing, but each time the hot pink hands vanished before I could touch them and tell them, *Stay away, I am not in need of saving.* I remained pristine, but the little fingers darkened and blistered all for my sake. Like kindling, they glowed an impossible orange even as they disintegrated into ash. Here is something strange about burning: the object is at its most brilliant in the very last moment—floating, flying, unquestionably alive.

CHAPTER 17 IN EVERY OPPOSITE

They said he was better, though he looked worse, thinner, more pallid than when he'd gone in. The sides of the gash had grown together again and the stitches had been removed. I was unsure about the hole in his lung, how such a thing might heal, but that was what they said: that he was better, getting better every day.

"He'll need a bit of TLC," said the nurse, smiling at him and then Lucy.

I walked beside my mother as she wheeled him down the white hospital corridor. Yes, he could walk, she whispered, but it was a rule that he leave this way.

To make us feel sorry, I thought.

That we now had to care for him sickened me. I could not look at him. I prayed he would not speak because I knew I could not bear to hear his voice, even his breathing, which made me think of the lung and how the hole had come about. And now he would always be with us. The three of us, that was how it would be. It was hard to believe that having him near was what I'd so badly wanted just weeks before. Wishing for that long drive and the drive-through. That if I had not wanted it, I would never have got in the car.

Though I knew it would happen, I was speechless when he came into our home below ground and slept in the big bed with Lucy.

"We need to all be together now," she told me. "All of us are hurting inside."

Him too, she meant, and so here he was, with us once more. There was not the laughter nor the fights of those earlier times. Only a long, dark silence that came to have a sound of its own. I lay listening to that, not sleeping. Afraid to sleep, because I had never slept alone before.

As soon as he returned, I returned to school, though Lucy said I could not possibly be ready, and that we would be leaving soon anyway, moving home. She said if I wanted to, I could take the rest of the term off. I could not conceive of a less bearable existence than being there—anywhere—with them, day after day, packing or discarding the things we had collected to fill a make-believe home.

In the mornings he stood in the kitchen. From my bed I could see him without looking right at him. He was wearing her pyjamas, which had once been his and had been reclaimed.

"Hi," he said, holding up a flat hand.

I ignored him. Moved cringing around him as I readied myself for school, avoiding the sleep-heated air that hung around his body. I prepared cereal, which I ate back in bed, facing away from him. But I could hear him chewing. I could hear the breath whistling from his nose. I could smell the peanut butter, which he ate every morning on barely toasted bread. He had always done this, but he was a different man than the one I had loved and lived with before. When he came near me I could feel that whole side of my body prickle and tense. It seemed a great wrong that he should be here when Eugenie was not.

Now I kept my eyes lowered always. I dressed in the bathroom and when I emerged I did not look up, not at him nor at her. When she walked with me to the door and kissed my face and pulled my hat on, still I did not look up.

"Bye," she said, handing me my lunch pail.

And he said, "See you later, Alligator." Those were his nonchalant words.

I walked alone to the bus stop. I stood alone in the snow. In class I sat without my sister beside me. At lunch

I ate alone. I thought I could feel everyone staring, and yet at the same time I felt invisible. If I did not look up, there was the chance they would not come near me. I was a flying squirrel, who lifts his tail to hide his face. Anyway, it was Eugenie who had talked and laughed with the others. Without her there was nothing to say. So I sat and stared at the table. At my hands. This lunch pail, it had all of the Archies on the cover, not just the stars but Big Ethel and Moose, everyone. I ran my hand over their comical faces and opened the lid. Inside was a sandwich in wax paper. I knew from the too-precise fold that Lucy had not wrapped it. I sat staring at what he'd touched. The tears that landed on the white wax paper looked just like glass, unmoving.

On the way home I dawdled. I stopped and sat on a hard grey snowbank and opened the lunch pail. With my thumb and finger I reached in and lifted the sandwich. Lifting like lifting a rotted fruit peel, my fingers arching out. I unfolded the paper and began to break the food into pieces. The pigeons as they landed were beautiful.

Every day I came home from school and saw that they had gotten rid of more of the things we had acquired. The empty picture frames and the long table that had once been someone's door. On the last day they dragged out the beanbag chair and left it by the side of the road.

"That was where we found it, after all," said Lucy. "It's good to give back what you get."

But I had never known anything so comfortable. When I had first sat in it I'd wondered why all chairs weren't made from beans. When you rose the shape of you stayed behind, just waiting for you to come back again. The stiff chairs at our other home would not show the indentation of our bodies this way.

"Won't it be good to be home?" said Lucy, hugging me.

No, it will not. It will not ever be good to be home.

We moved back in the coming of spring, the opposite of moving away. In every opposite there is a connection. Still the bright white birch trees gleamed, as they had that day with Eugenie.

He and Lucy wanted to play a game, to spy with our little eye something that was grey, green, blue, but I could not move my eyes at will, and when I tried to focus on something, I found that I was not looking at the object but at the space, the air between me and that object, where seemingly there was nothing. When it was Lucy's turn, I stayed quiet and let him do all the guessing. When it was his turn, I let Lucy. When it was my turn, I didn't spy anything. I leaned back and closed my eyes and said, "I spy with my little eye something that is red," and as they guessed and guessed I thought of the red apples we had eaten in such delicious secret, the ribbons we had tied to our braids when our hair had been long enough for weaving, the boots that had matched her purple ones and that had long ago disappeared, and Red Cap, I thought of Red Cap too.

I had been sleeping, upright and belted in. My head had tried to rest on my own shoulder and my neck ached.

When I woke my father's face was right in front of mine, the guilty eyes filled up with my guilty reflection. Him and me there, just the two of us.

"Ssshhh," he said. "It's okay," and I thought I must have been talking in my sleep, but already whatever I'd dreamed of had slipped away.

He smiled, and there was such warmth in it. It had been forever since I had looked into his grieving face. He was placing a blanket over me, tucking it in, and when he had finished he pressed his foreign lips to my forehead. I shut my eyes against him and in a moment he was back in the driver's seat and we were once more on our way.

Blue had been left with Miss Reese. In my father's absence, he had dug through her carpet and gouged the floor below, and now he was chained to a tree in her backyard because he could not be trusted to behave. It was just where he'd been that day of my drowning. There was nowhere he could sit but in melting snow, and when

I first saw him he was facing away from me, sitting but not, his poor cold haunches lifted just above the ground. I thought that the pads of his black-and-pink paws, which made him seem almost human, must be frozen right through, because today was wet and grey, not a day like spring. I moved towards him with my hand out. He turned and began to wag his tail and tried to keep the rest of his body from moving with it. He could see it was me, or one of us. He pulled and pulled, choking himself with the chain, and when I got to him he did what he was taught not to and stood on his hind legs with his paws on my shoulders. I pressed my face into his wet-dog smell and I blew into his mouth to make him lick me. That was when I cried. I cried as I bent in the dirty trampled snow where he'd been made to stay, and I cried as I unclasped his leash from the tree and saw the scars it had left on the bark.

Miss Reese saw me from the window. I watched her hand flutter to her mouth. She disappeared and then reappeared at the door, coming to me coatless in her slippers.

"Oh, Bunny," she said, and it made me cry harder. She helped me into the house and sat me in that big red chair. She let Blue, wet and dirty, stay with me.

"Let it all out," she told me, as though crying was like vomiting—if you did it for long enough, you got to the end.

In the spring I took Eugenie's ashes to Pine Point Beach, near Uncle William's house. I squatted in the wet sand at the river's edge, where we had built sandcastles, and let the ice-cold water rush over my feet, covering, uncovering them. My reflection moved with the waves. I thought of how the water might mix with the fine dry ash and I thought of seamonkeys, nothing but dust in a little paper packet, or hope. They were meant to come alive when we submerged them, though they never did, not once. This was not like that. There was no hope in me. I opened the urn and tipped it. The ashes poured out in a stream of fine grey sand, not in a puffball cloud, the way I had expected. They lingered in the water for only an instant, and then they were gone forever.

What I did not yet know was that Eugenie lived on in multiple somewheres. Her eyes, her mysterious insides. Whatever they wanted they took from her. Years later, when I was told, I thought of how, eyeless, heartless, she had burned to ash. And then I thought, Someone sees through her eyes.

CHAPTER 18 SEE-SAW

In telling you this story, I recall my room without my sister, the bunk beds and the posters on the wall which she had hung all at the same crooked angle. There I was again. And what can you do about bunk beds? One depends on the other, thus they take time to dismantle, and effort, and in the meantime they are so big and obvious, you can never get away from them. He and Lucy must have thought the beds upset me, that it would be better for me if my sister's bed was gone, but I was never asked, and the day that I came into my room and saw it not there was a turbulent day. What I can remember is opening my mouth and screaming. All the books in my arms fell and the loose pages fluttered out, see-sawing to the floor. I screamed not frightened screams but wild, angry screams. Lucy was there in an instant and had me by the shoulders, shaking me, but I couldn't stop. I put my whole splayed hand on her face and I pushed hard to push her away. I can see it now, my little hand on her hot blushing skin. She fell backwards and sat in a ball on the floor, crying, and I moved around my room, swiping my hand across the shelves that held our exquisite things: the horse, ceramic because we could not have a real one, the flowery bone-china tea set, meant not for us but for dolls, cups like thimbles. Everything flew and smashed in a glorious mess. And then I sank to the floor.

I don't know how long we stayed among the many smithereens, but he found us there. He came and stood in the doorway. I did not look up, but I could see him in the periphery. He had his hands on the door frame. It seemed a long time before he stepped into the room. He went to Lucy first, bent, stroked her hair and kissed her. And then he came to me. In his shoes he walked across the broken pieces. He slid one arm around my back and the other under my knees and he lifted me, and I can't tell you how that felt, dissolving into him. I leaned against his shoulder and I cried, quietly now. The strength of his arms. The faded sky blue of his shirt, many times washed and worn. It was an impossible, unforgettable moment.

You should have seen the children stare at me. Stare, and look away. For days when I first returned to school, no one who was not an adult spoke to me. Not one word, *Hello, I'm sorry*, not even from Rebecca, who had been our closest friend. It was as though I was dead too, they'd just forgotten to burn me. And surely I looked emptier than I ever had. Empty of food, of feeling. I combed my hair straight down, no barrettes, no elastics, for I could shake it onto my face this way, me a pony with blinders. More than once I wondered how they would treat Eugenie if she had lost me, and I could see them all clearly in my mind, huddled around her, taking her hand. And for some reason she was wearing her hair in exuberant pigtails, more alive in my mind's eye than I was in my own breathing body.

Yet everyone was curious. I was an anomaly now, a twinless twin, a rumour. Everywhere I went the whispers flew behind and above me. And then when my eyes met theirs, a cold dead silence.

Alone, I turned eleven.

Every day after school I wandered not home but to Uncle William's. I cannot even say that it was a conscious decision on my part but rather as though a magnet pulled me there, fulfilling my unwitting need to be somewhere safe and serene. The large window looked out on the navy Ottawa River. If you sat there, Simon, and saw it, you would think of some famous Canadian painting. The way the light falls. The flat slanted rocks and the trees. Despite my intimate knowledge of Emily Carr, at the time I knew nothing of Tom Thomson or the Group of Seven. To me, this was Uncle William's land, set apart from the town, wild but so tame. Up from the sand and the rock grew jack pines, hungry trees with scarred trunks, their needles almost black from a distance. Even in clusters these were the lonely trees, the true trees of sadness, though in myth it was the perfect symmetrical cypress that owned that name. I, like the jack pine, was starving. Skin and bone. Eleven, and growing taller every day, my knees and elbows bulging.

Every afternoon I sat on the deck looking out at the river. Uncle William offered the sweet chocolate fingers of ladies, which my sister and I had loved to devour. I smiled my thank-you, and Uncle William left me alone. The fingers were arranged in a splaying circle as though they were the sun's rays or the petals of a daisy. I was a million years too old for that now. One by one I dropped them into the dark spaces between the deck's wooden slats, treats for the raccoons and the chipmunks, for the squirrels who chewed on the wires in Uncle William's walls and thus had to be trapped like mice or vile city rats. I didn't care about that any more, the way I once had. When I came upon a trap, I could look with indifference at the still body and the small pointed face with its open black eyes. I could see where the metal had slammed closed on the red-fur neck, and to care less would have been to simply not notice at all.

And yet I fed them. I dropped the morsels down into the negative space and how could I not recall my sister, who had fed the creatures dwelling in that violent hole in the wall of our home?

Lucy had taught us of negative space, a lesson that had come from her art class. She said it was a whole new way of seeing, and all you had to do was look at what wasn't there. So not the wood of the deck but the slats made from nothing. Not my ten toes but the spaces, only eight, between them. Not the leaves of this birch tree but the air around them, visible for those who looked long enough. And not me but Eugenie.

I dropped another finger into the darkness below the deck. I could not savour any food. The more delicious a morsel might be, the more it sickened me to think of tasting or even smelling it.

Every day at five o'clock, one of them came to get me. If it was he, we drove home in silence, and if it was she, she chatted non-stop: What did you do? What did you learn? Did you make a new friend? How are you feeling? Oh, Janie, I love you, do you know? Which was nearly unbearable, perhaps even as unbearable as when my father came for me, for now I saw myself reflected when

I looked in his eyes, and I was abhorrent there. I saw the awful night, a culmination of many awful times, and I saw myself plead, "Genie, please, let's go." I saw the jelly-bean cake and I saw the two of us—myself and my father—conspirators in an ugly crime. Up close, I saw his neck as I hugged him that night and I felt his desperate breath on my skin as he whispered, "I want you to come home, I want you all home." The smell of him both repugnant and magnetic, lost for so long. Somewhere in the room Eugenie stood alive at that moment. Blood pumped from her heart and circled through her and her pink lungs breathed and released air. If we could time-lapse that moment, the way they do with flowers, per-haps we would even see her growing.

What I would have preferred was that neither of them came for me, but rather let me live on with Uncle William and the river and the birds, both the ones who flew and the ones who slept in the polished wooden boxes.

Once when Lucy came to bring me home—this only months after Eugenie's death—I heard the car pull up but she did not immediately appear on the deck. I wait-ed, watching the smooth summer water. I did not go to her now, not ever. I waited for her to come to me. Just barely could I hear her voice and Uncle William's. I watched a squirrel run along the rail of the deck, up a tree and out of sight. In the distance a canoe was get-ting smaller. I heard their voices for a long time. When the canoe had disappeared altogether I stood and moved towards the door of the house. I pressed my face against the screen. Uncle William was holding her and she was crying.

"You don't have to stay with him," he said.

I could see her back shaking.

"Really," he said, holding her shoulders and looking into her face. "You don't have to stay."

It was almost imperceptible, but I heard her.

"Yes, I do," she said. "I love him."

This was the see-saw of love, the one we had always been riding. And right in the middle of that old conundrum of horrible love I was faced with a new conundrum: people can change, yes, but will it change anything? I never saw my father take another drink in the ensuing years. Not once did he raise his voice to me or to Lucy, at least not in my presence. Now, on the rare occasions that he became angry, he folded in on himself. The vein in his forehead still throbbed but he said nothing. I found his silence alarming, at times more frightening than the outbursts had been. The pressure mounting inside of him was never released, but I could not believe that it disappeared, thus every quiet time seemed more dangerous than the last.

The funny thing was that time kept passing. I remained unchanged but outside the river was trying to freeze and all the fish were catching cold, swimming deeper. Slowly, the water pulled a blanket of ice over itself to keep out the torture of winter.

In January, nearly a year after my sister's death, I began my first whole year without her. As a family we went to Uncle William's on New Year's Eve, the way we had most every year except the last one. I was allowed to bring a friend but I wanted no one. Guy Lombardo was long gone, but on television they still released balloons at midnight, and again the story was told that Uncle William had delivered a package to the Lombardo family when he was a boy in London, Ontario; that he had arrived just as dinner was to be served, and so been invited in. Guy Lombardo was only an ordinary boy then, there was nothing famous about him. But everyone clung to the story, and once we had too, Eugenie and me. We were proud to know of Uncle William's gossamer connection with fame. Picturing him little in knickers and a hat. And who could not invite Uncle William for dinner were he to appear at the door? That was what we thought. Surely he had been as wonderful then as now, smiling and bursting with stories. Every year we asked about the Lombardos: What he had eaten there, how long he had stayed, and what had been in the package he'd brought. But this new year I was nauseous. How dare we try to make it the same as the others, wearing our garish paper hats and blowing our horns, telling all the same old stories.

At midnight my father kissed my mother and swung her around, hugging her so tightly her paper hat crumpled. On the toes of Uncle William's good shoes I was dancing to the sweetest music this side of heaven, that's what Guy called it, and I was hoping Lucy and Dad would not come for me, though of course, of course they did. They were my mother and father. They wrapped their four arms around me, and Uncle William his two, and I was like the prey of an insect until they released me and we split in half again, two and two. I leaned against Uncle William. He turned me in circles to the music of "Auld Lang Syne," a song that seemed to be about forgetting. Outside the trees and the ground and the river were wearing their best bright white, so easily spoiled. My mother and father had been dancing in this room for twice as long as I had lived. I could see them now as children, holding each other with their thin, tentative arms, and for the smallest midnight moment, I understood.

Do you know he must have been almost like her brother, and she, his sister? Twelve years old they were when they met. He the lonely child of unsmiling parents, and she—who knew who she was? Anne of Green Gables. Whatever had gone wrong and landed her with Uncle William she would not ever say. That it had been tragic and unfair was only my guess. That it had been a blessing—a welcoming place to land—was undeniable. Lucy's room had been across the hall from Uncle

William's, overlooking the ongoing trees instead of the water. I escaped there now that midnight was over. I opened the window and welcomed the brutal air of winter. At night, away from artificial light, the world is like a black-and-white movie, have you noticed? Everything made from shades of grey. Some of the charcoal leaves hung heavy with snow, which was falling in fat cartoon flakes from the sky.

What was left of Lucy's childhood was somewhere in this room. A picture on the dresser showed what she looked like the year she arrived here. Laughing, a live bird on her shoulder. The picture was already old the first time I saw it, but I remember that the circle scar on her forehead was more apparent in that image. Grown over, but a recent wound. We looked at that photo a lot as children, saying nothing to each other as we stared and fogged the glass with our breath. I thought of that alone on New Year's Eve. I walked to the dresser, held the frame in my hand and blew the dust from it. I touched the tender spot with my finger.

Every month at school we learned the reason behind that month's name. I was paying attention. I wanted to learn everything I could, to eat the stories and keep them inside me. January had long ago been named for Janus, god of doorways and gates, of beginnings and endings. The growing-up god, he pushed you from childhood

to adulthood, whether or not you wanted to go. He
pushed you from peace into war, and war into peace.
God of transition, he was with you when you planted a
seed in the earth and again when you sowed it. He was
there for your birth, for your marriage, for the birth of
your own child. God of the connection of opposites, he
was the tightrope between country and city, barbarism
and sophistication. From my desk he looked up at me,
almost winking. I touched his xeroxed image, his formidable double face. Two faces, you see. One to look back
and one to look forward.

I became twelve and thirteen. There is this saying, *Life
goes on*, and it's true. But what use is it to tell you of the
normal times? The pass the sugar, what is for dinner,
what's on TV days? There were those. It was not all this
poignant way. But what is memory if not summary, the
sum of a life? In all, it was a bleak time, without the pretty edges of melancholy. But yes, I laughed and seemed an
average girl one Thursday, or maybe for a summer or a
year. I wrote a poem and won a prize. I kissed a boy with
brown eyes and thought it meant love. I learned to play
the clarinet and I sat with the band, one among many, a
single normal girl, knowing always, bone-deep, that
nothing could ever be normal about me now or ever, no
matter how I pretended. So I pass that by, in my memory,
and here as I tell it to you. What I can give you of that

time is the distillation, only the essence, which after all is essential, all that matters when the rest is gone and cannot be revived. This is what it tastes like for me, this strong. This is how pungent it smells.

Uncle William died when I was seventeen. There was nothing horrible about it. He was an old man. To me, he had been old when I was born. He used to joke that he had been born in the dinosaur age, that he loved birds so much because they resembled miniature dinosaurs with their backwards-bending legs; they reminded him of his childhood. Perhaps he was the true descendant of the archaeopteryx, a word that had sounded complicated the first time he'd told us, and then so simple when he'd spoken the translation: ancient wing. He had shown us a picture of the fossil skeleton of that rare and primitive bird, and we were amazed by how clear an imprint could be after hundreds of millions of years. We could see the skull and the curved turkey neck, the clawed hands and feet and the delicate, barely visible feathers.

Uncle William died on an ordinary summer night, in his sleep. No fossils that told of him would be found among the flat rocks or deep in the coarse sand of Pine Point, but for me that place would always exude him. As he grew drowsy, the last thing he would have seen, surely, was the view from his bedroom window. The jack pine rising black against the blue velvet sky, perhaps a star falling. Through his screen he would have certainly heard the waves spilling up on the shore. Summer wind in the paper-thin birch leaves. No sign of struggle, only Uncle William sleeping on and on, a flannel sheet pulled over him to keep the chill off. His chest rising and falling and rising no more. I would miss him. I had loved him, but I was not mournful or angry that he was gone now, for this was a right death, appropriate. A life lived full and happy. How much he had given, how good he had been. He had everything to be proud of now.

And yet what it signalled for me was that I, too, was finished here. Without him there was nothing to hold me but one final year of school, a fall, a winter, a spring, which at the time seemed interminable, but I told myself, *Think of how many seasons you have endured here already. One more, you can do it.*

And of course I left on the bus, it's the only way you can leave Deep River unless you own a car or you hitch-hike. There I was looking out at them, Lucy, Dad, Miss Reese and Blue. All of them thinking of the other times, no doubt, and me thinking only of the enormous future. They wanted and did not want me to go, I could see that. Wishing everything for me, a big life brimming over. And in a way I had left them so long ago that this good-bye was a mere formality.

A new century has dawned in my absence. I cannot say whether or not I knew at the time that more than a decade would pass before I returned. It was not a conscious decision. And yet without question, I knew that as soon as it was possible, I wanted to be far away.

In Sudbury, I boarded a train that took me further west, and through the thick trees I watched the landscape I had known forever fade slowly into prairie. And then the brown Rocky Mountains, harsh and ominous, mellowed only by the green water snaking through them. Sleeping dinosaur mountains, with wrinkled backs and hidden faces. From there to British Columbia. Everything moist and shining, soaked in green. Right away I thought I would never leave. When I arrived in Vancouver, I could smell the ocean and everywhere I looked people were smiling. I believed I would lose myself there. It was everything I wanted.

And the rest you know, Simon. Of my one-room apartment in Chinatown, my fruit-selling first job on Granville Island, my years at school, and every spare moment, my stories, which brought me to you.

CHAPTER 19 A CIRCLE

I pack my bag, say goodbye to Dolores and walk to the bus station. There is a smell in the air, the dying of winter, because in the city winter ends earlier than elsewhere. I look at all the garbage released from the melting February snow, plastic bags caught in trees. The leafless hanging branches of the willows are yellow now, preparing for spring. Yellow too are the feet of the gulls, pressed flat against their bodies as they fly. Lucy used to say those were their rain boots, because our own rain boots were yellow ones, year after year, to cheer us on days that were dreary.

"Yellow is the colour of spring," she said.

"Why not green?" we asked. "Shouldn't green be the colour of spring?"

"Heavens no! All the green things in spring have a yellowish cast long before they turn truly green. Haven't you ever noticed? Yellow is a sign that something good is coming."

I'm spying yellow now, with my little eye. On a bus headed backwards and forwards.

"Please come," he had said on the phone, but his voice had not held the desperation of those earlier years. He was calling for her, not himself, though we both knew acutely that once she was gone we would only have each other.

My father's name is David. David Michael Ingrams. As I have said, he has eyes that are both blue and green at once, which means they are neither. Mine are that colour, and so were my sister's. He was twelve years old when he fell in love with my mother. She was spinning in cartwheels from one end of the football field to the other. It was Sunday, there was no one around. He stood on the hill and watched her twirling. The backdrop was the still Ottawa River, from which a thick mist rose, and beyond that, the Laurentian Mountains, which he could not see that day. He knew the rise and fall of them, though the fog veiled their shape and the ever-changing shades of autumn, repeated every year. It was a windless, colourless morning, but the cartwheeling girl was dressed in golden yellow. With her flying orange hair she was the colour of the missing sun, or fire. She spun and spun, until she reached the goalposts. There she stopped abruptly, stood with her arms in the air and wavered, as though some unseen version of herself had not stopped reeling but was actively cartwheeling back the other way, hands, feet, hands, feet. He was dizzy with her. He watched her free-fall backwards to the ground. In the calm moist air she giggled, and her echo bounced on the water.

Until that moment, he had been a quiet, friendless boy, but he smiled, watching her.

Though I did not know my father when he was twelve years old, I see him just the same. The expression on his face tells not just this story, of their meeting, but many more that come after. If he could look back and see what I see—his smiling self on this hill—he might remember and believe in extrasensory perception, because at this moment he has that extra sense, is seeing Lucy for the first time and being thrust forward to a day when he will touch her skin and lie beside her, breathing in the apple smell of her long loose hair. He is seeing ahead to another day, far off, when her belly is a balloon and she is not even nervous but elated, laughing and telling him, *You're too serious, everything will be okay,* and there is something almost violent rising up in him at her casual response.

Nevertheless, she is right, everything is okay. The delicate babies who emerge are mirror-image twins, not one miracle, but two. One in each crook of her arm, they are sleeping. He is sitting close, on the edge of the bed, looking from one to the other. Lucy is non-stop chatting to both Jane and Eugenie, newly named, but he, he is speechless.

"Yoo-hoo," Lucy calls, laughing. "Come back—you're over the moon!"

And he is.

In spite of this, he has never been so frightened.

From the time that we were babies, my mother recited the story of Millie-Christine, eighth wonder of the world.

"One wonder?" we asked. "Or two?"

Lucy paused, then shrugged. "Two, I suppose. Technically, anyway. But Millie-Christine's own mother, Monemia, referred to the two babies in the singular. Her big, perfect girl."

We didn't know whether this failure to distinguish was right or wrong, for Lucy didn't say. Regardless, I adored Monemia. Her mellifluous name and her fervour. The huge double baby—seventeen pounds—spilled out of her as easily as the many single ones she had borne already. And she was inconsolable when Millie-Christine was kidnapped. She could not eat or sleep. People said it was impossible that such a conspicuous child, merged at the base of the spine, could utterly vanish, but Monemia, mother of a wonder, knew all things were possible.

We treasured every telling because it was the perfect story, a circle, complete with singing and dancing and meeting the queen. The wondrous double heroine, miraculously borne by a loving slave mother. The heightened moment of dismay, when Millie-Christine was who-knows-where in the underground world of the circus. The wash of relief when she was finally, wholly, returned.

Trading cards were made in her honour. She was called the eighth wonder of the world, so astonishing was she, and also the two-headed nightingale for the beauty of her song, which was two songs, sung in soprano and contralto, a harmony.

You may now make new sense of the stories, Simon. Of the rainbow parable of One and Tother, which at the time you teased me about, calling it "another one of your affliction stories." It was my cryptic way of telling you about Eugenie, though of course it told you nothing at all. You drew the little girls never knowing you were drawing me and my sister, just as in *Miss Hummingbird* you drew us—me and you—and it made me feel worse, not better, to maintain my silence in the shadow of your playful depictions. Yet I suppose you must have seen us in this story. You knew it was us, but you didn't know why. The craziest thing of all is that the truth is so much easier to tell than I ever thought it could be. I cannot explain why I never told you before, except to say that twins who lose a twin are always looking, lost too. I looked and looked and what I found was you.

Miss Hummingbird and the Long-Armed Stranger

Once there was a woman who was always lying. She was an old woman, and she had been lying almost all of her life, but no one listened, so in a way it didn't matter. People passed right by her and looked right through her as she spouted her lies. She told them she lived in the CN Tower, and she pointed at it with her grubby finger. "That's my house," she said, "but I'm hardly ever there because it's always spinning, spinning, spinning, and boy, do I get dizzy. I've got vertigo, you know? And I can't find the switch to stop the thing from whirling around."

In reality, she lived who-knew-where, in an intangible land making up stories. She was ever so skinny, but she was full to the brim with lies.

"You shouldn't come too close to me," she told the people who criss-crossed in front of her in their dress-up clothes and their click-clack shoes. "Spontaneous combustion runs in my family."

The thing she despised most was to have people close to her. She found that when they came too near, even if their distracted busy faces were pointed away from her, each individual hair on her body stood on guard and aimed at them, and she developed purple goose bumps. Her heart beat just a little faster than normal (and normal, for her, was very rapid indeed). She began to sweat, and her breath came in short panicky gasps.

"I have a lot of things that are catching," she'd say in a louder voice, though to whom it was not clear. No one slowed long enough to hear the whole sentence. "Measles, for instance. They're just beginning to form under my arms and behind my knees, and here, below my hairline. I'd show you, but it's cold out and I'm susceptible to the cold." She poked a finger up under her toque and scratched herself, though of course there was not one measly measle upon her. In the near cosmopolitan distance, people hurried by. "For your own good, keep away!" she shouted, cupping her hands around her mouth. "Plus, I'm always fighting the flu, you know, ever since I was a baby. When I was just newly born, all of my blood was drained out of me at the hospital in a terrible patient mix-up, oh, I don't often speak of it, but when they put the blood back in they didn't give me quite enough, which is why I am hyperanemic."

"Ha!" she heard. "Crrrap!"

But where had it come from?

Bewildered, she looked around. A squatting man had perched himself on top of a nearby mailbox, and was sneering at her.

"I beg your pardon?" she asked, holding her hand up as though to keep him at bay as she spoke.

"I said, 'Crrrap!'" he told her. He curled his lips back to reveal huge yellow teeth. "Everything you say is a big fat lie."

"You better get lost!" she said, pointing at him with a shaking finger. "You're in a lot of danger even this far away, do you understand?" She turned her finger towards herself now, and knocked at her own chest with it. "I have cholera and the mumps," she said.

The man gave a snorting laugh. He hooked his arm around the telephone pole beside him and leaned closer. "Crrrap!" he said again, showing the teeth.

All of her hairs were pointing at him, willing him away, but he continued to come closer. He leaned so far towards her that his arm, the one holding the telephone pole, stretched like Plasticene.

"Stand back!" she shouted, but instead he leaped from the mailbox and landed on the sidewalk beside her. A foul odour came with him.

"You smell," she said, wrinkling her wrinkled nose.

"It's a tonic I wear," he said, and grinned widely. "It keeps me from catching absolutely everything." And he reached out and squeezed her nose with his thumb and finger.

The strangest thing happened to the place he had touched: it went all warm and tingly, a sensation that began to spread through the rest of her face and down into her body. She touched her nose in alarm and glared at him.

"Stand back!" she said again, though less forcefully. She could see her sticking-up hair and her maniacal expression in his eye. How little she looked, a dwarf inside her too-big coat and her anger.

He settled down beside her, and nothing she could say or do would get rid of him. He talked long into the evening, of ungulates who chewed in a circle, of elephants who cried and of sloths who moved so rarely, so slowly, that they gathered moss—all true tales that had the musical ring of stories. He spoke in a very quiet voice—a voice unlike the one that had shouted "Crrrap" at her—and she found herself moving closer to him to hear what he had to say.

But he had stopped speaking.

"What is that sound?" he asked finally.

It might have been a hundred cars passing, or the streetcars hurtling east, west, north and south, or a man singing or a truck idling or a dog whining or a baby screaming or a horn honking or a thousand feet stepping or a door slamming, but it was not.

"It's your heart beating," he said.

For a moment they simply looked at each other and listened.

"I've never heard anything like it," he told her. "Well, not in a human, anyway, but you should hear the heart of a hummingbird!" He made a rapid vibrational whir with his tongue against his top lip. "Five hundred beats per minute, I kid you not. And what a perilous existence! By the end of the day the tiny heart is so worn out it barely beats through the night. Sometimes it stops completely and the bird just dies." He looked at the old woman gravely. "You ought to be careful with a heart like yours, Miss Hummingbird."

Every morning when she woke she saw the fringes of his jacket disappearing around the corner. She wondered if he stayed all night because of her precarious heart, and the pleasant thought of his vigil carried her through the hollow, populous daytime.

By late afternoon he appeared without fail in a new and surprising spot: inside the garbage bin, peering out, or stick-thin behind the telephone pole, windmilling his overlong arms, and once, most astonishingly, swinging from the curve of the street lamp.

"How did you get up there?" she asked.

"Like this," he said, and let go. She watched the stunt in slow motion, his dirty shoes growing huge like a clown's as they flew through the air towards her, and then shrinking and landing in front of her with a sound as small as a child's footstep. "Like that," he said, "but backwards."

The woman's old lying mouth dropped open and he reached forward and closed it. "You should try it some time. Spread your wings a bit."

The place where he touched her—the tip of her chin—was tingling now, the way her nose had when he'd pinched it.

Gentle pins and needles spread through her in a wash unlike the purple goose bumps. They tickled her sad old bod, and she smiled in response, though only with one side of her mouth.

On the fourteenth night, she fell asleep with her head on his shoulder.

It was many blissful weeks after that that he began to tell her about his childhood home far north of here, about the gravel roads and the farmers' fields and the rocky cliffs and the rabbits and the chipmunks (which were little squirrels with stripes, he explained) and the spindly jack pines.

"Go on and on," she said, snuggling into him.

And so he told her about the sky where he came from, how it might one night be an enormous black dome studded silver with stars. "You'll never see that here," he told her. "All the smog and the man-made light covers up the starlight." He shook his head sadly and continued. Another night, the sky where he came from might be draped in long luminous bands of red and green. "The northern lights," he said. "You've never seen anything like it. Maybe you've seen a pretty pink sunset, but until you've seen this, you ain't seen nothin'. Once I saw half the sky go red. It was almost scary. It rippled like a sky made from blood and I thought it might start pouring red rain."

Every day when he left she fell back into her ranting and her lying, and a trillion preoccupied people milled this way and that, not heeding her. Perhaps she spoke with less enthusiasm now, for in truth she could no longer believe that she was dying, even ailing, not when late afternoon and evening was still to come, not when the happy thought of him hummed within her.

On the seventy-first night, he gave her a gift: a very smooth round stone that he had once skipped into the river and then retrieved for its uncommon beauty. It was grey, like most stones, but if you looked long enough at it, you could see how it was almost green. She held it in her palm and rubbed her thumb over it, unable to say anything at all.

She spent the whole of the seventy-second day wondering what to give him in return, but she had only her clothes, her big coat, her rainboots, her toque, her blanket and a bag full of newspapers and trinkets. She would have happily parted with any of these things if she thought they would please him, but surely they were nothing he needed or desired.

When he arrived, swinging with his long arms from street lamp to street lamp, her old hummingbird heart raced at the sight of him. He hung, smiling down at her with his huge yellow teeth, and she looked up and said, "Thank you. For yesterday, I mean, and the stone."

They settled into their familiar place on the sidewalk and watched the people hurry by. They were holding hands, and the stone was in both of their palms. He was stroking her thumb with his thumb.

"I wanted to give you something," she told him. "Just to thank you. But I'm afraid all of my things are in the tower, and I just can't face going back there again, not with my vertigo and my heart palp-palping the way it does."

His thumb stopped stroking her thumb. "You don't have to give me anything," he said.

"Oh, but I want to and would! And I really do have an array of things! It's just the spin-spin-spin and all the people and my dizzy—"

"It's okay," he said.

There was an awkward pause and he took his hand from hers and folded her fingers over the stone. He stood up and paced back and forth, and she said, sensing she had disappointed him, "I have a ruby-studded belt buckle in the tower, and it's yours the minute I am well enough to go back there. You mark my—"

"Really!" he said. "I don't want a gift. Look, I have no belt." And he pointed. "Plus all my pockets have holes in them. Whatever you give me would just fall right through." He stooped and scooped a pebble from the sidewalk, tucked it into his ear, then shook himself from head to toe and let it fall out of his pant leg. "See?" he said, but he only laughed a little.

She, meanwhile, was brimming with melancholy, and her heart was slowing down, though it was not yet night and time for sleeping.

He squatted beside her and held the hand with the stone again. "If you want to give me something, tell me about yourself. Go on and on. I want to know everything. Where are you really from? Why are you really here? Why do you lie all the time, even to me?"

But she did not look at him. She kept her old head bent forward and she pointed to the CN Tower, where a lit-up cable car climbed like a bug up its body. "I'm from there," she said.

"Crap," he said, but quietly. Without smiling, without rolling his *r*'s. "The trouble with you is, you will never understand the basic mechanics of the see-saw."

She could not look up to see him leaving. She kept her head down and waited for night, so dependable, and for the paltry stars and the artificial light from the street lamps and the inevitable slowing of her humming frantic heart.

*

It is night and the Greyhound bus is rushing alone down the highway. Through the side windows black pine trees blur against a blue-black sky. I am the only passenger left on the bus, which soon rolls to a sighing stop. I am wide awake, but unmoving. The driver stands and walks towards me in the dark, perhaps expecting I am sleeping.

"Ma'am?" he says. "Deep River."

And just like before—the chairlift, the plane—I am made to get off, go forward, so back. The cold air shocks my lungs when I step outside. All of a sudden I am here, and all I can think is, Oh God, how strange. That time can move so slowly you don't even notice it going by, but it tricks you. Other than dying, there's nothing you can ever do to stop it.

So here I am walking in improper boots through the snow, which is soft but dense, freshly fallen. There is no one on the street. It is dark, and very late. An odd quiet hovers over the town, as though a storm has just blown through. Stars are beginning to appear.

I follow the road that runs parallel to the frozen river. The only sound is my heart and my footsteps squeaking in the snow. There is not even wind. All the way I drag my suitcase. It ploughs through the snow behind me, erasing one footprint. I am both afraid and so calm. What surprises me most is that my heart is enormous inside me. I can feel it pumping against my chest wall, I can feel my mouth smiling.

Long before I knock, the door swings open. And now I have gone as far as I will go from you, Simon, which means that I am halfway home.

ACKNOWLEDGMENTS

Some of the stories Lucy tells the twins originally came to me through two books: *The Mystery and Lore of Monsters* by C.J.S. Thompson and *The Curious World of Twins* by Vincent and Margaret Gaddis.

Ever so gratefully, I acknowledge the financial assistance of the Canada Council for the Arts.

For countless reasons, thanks to William Cartwright, my grandfather; Siobhan Maloney; Julie Trimingham; Deborah Mills; Reed and Caitlin Russell; Paula Fullerton; Sara Angelucci; Ian Cauthery; Jennifer Billinsky; Adrienne Elson; Lynne Nicolson; and Kate Yorga. Thanks also to James Hall and Gabrielle Stannus, who shared their tomatoes and took excellent care of the King of Spain; Chip himself; Janet Hardy, whose drawings grace these pages, and David Blostein, enthusiastic critic of early versions of *The Perpetual Ending*. I am indebted to my exacting agent, Denise Bukowski, who wrote "Huh?" in the margins when I wasn't making sense, and to my editors Diane Martin and Noelle Zitzer, fellow believers in the importance of make-believe. Once again, tremendous support and inspiration came my way from Mom, Dad, George, Helen, Tracy, Gene, Heidi, Colin, Sophia, Ethan, Chloe and a little trillium called Christopher William. "But why?" he asks. "Kee-kuzz," I say. And finally, to Robert Boyd: *Posso solamente dirti. . .* thank you, Mister.

KRISTEN DEN HARTOG is the author of the acclaimed novel *Water Wings*. Her writing has also appeared in numerous magazines, journals and anthologies. She is currently working on her third novel, and divides her time between Toronto and the Ottawa Valley.